GW01463840

THE LEGEND OF INJUN JOE BRADY

The Legend of Injun Joe Brady

J.D. KINCAID

A Black Horse Western

ROBERT HALE · LONDON

© J.D. Kincaid 1996
First published in Great Britain 1996

ISBN 0 7090 5924 8

Robert Hale Limited
Clerkenwell House
Clerkenwell Green
London EC1R 0HT

Photoset in North Wales by
Derek Doyle & Associates, Mold, Clwyd.
Printed and bound in Great Britain by
WBC Book Manufacturers Limited,
Bridgend, Mid-Glamorgan.

ONE

It was Saturday night and Chuck Leney had ridden into Great Falls, as was his custom on that particular night of the week. He was mighty glad to leave his roan at the livery stables and hurry into the warmth of Mooney's Saloon. Although it was mid-April, the winter of 1883 had been unusually severe and the State of Montana remained chill and bleak. There was still snow on the mountain-tops and not all of the passes were open.

Leney was a big man and a rich man. He owned the Triple L spread, several hundred thousand acres of prime cattle country to the east of Great Falls. A man in his early forties, he had married late in life and now had three children, the eldest of whom was just five years old. Domesticity did not suit him, however, and he had changed few of his bachelor habits. Attendance at the Saturday night poker game was one of the many he had retained.

5

Throwing open his heavy sheepskin coat, the rancher strode purposefully across the bar-room to the bar with its marbled top and enormous, splendidly engraved mirror. He ordered a whiskey and turned to survey the scene. He was an imposing figure: tall, wide-shouldered and broad-chested, with thick, steel-grey hair, cool blue eyes, a large Roman nose, hard mouth and firm, square jaw. The low-crowned grey Stetson, the fine white cambric shirt with its ruffed collar, the black coat, the dark-grey trousers and the gleaming black leather boots were what Chuck Leney called his Sunday best, although in fact he never attended church and reserved the wearing of these clothes solely for his poker nights at Mooney's Saloon.

In a holster on his right thigh, he carried a Remington. No gunman, Leney hadn't bothered to carry a handgun for quite a spell. Then, a little over three years ago, he had taken to wearing a revolver. Several of his friends had commented on this fact, but had elicited no explanation from the rancher.

As Leney sipped his whiskey, he noted that the usual crowd sat round the big table in the centre of the bar-room. Saturday nights at Mooney's varied little. Faro, blackjack and poker were all on offer, as were the services of Noel Mooney's sporting women, five in all, including a recent addition, a voluptuous redhead, with an Irish lilt

6

and an Irish name, called Bonnie Regan. Leney
caught the redhead's eye and smiled. Then he
transferred his gaze to the big table. It was round
this that the high-rollers sat. Only the really
well-heeled could afford the stakes played for at
the big table. The rest of Great Falls' citizenry had
to content themselves with the games of chance
on offer at the other, smaller tables.

Chuck Leney finished his whiskey, then
ordered another and strolled across to the big
table. He was feeling lucky and poker was his
game.

'Howdy, boys. Mind if I sit in?' he growled.

'Hell, no! Draw up a chair an' sit yoreself down,
Chuck,' said James Higgins, an elegant, silver-
haired man who, besides being Great Falls'
leading businessman, was also its elected mayor.

Like Higgins, the other poker players were all
men whom Chuck Leney knew well: the banker,
Fletcher Mulgrove; Dan Freestone, the hotelier; a
couple of fellow-ranchers; Bill Hartley who was
big in real estate; Indian agent, Tim Rowe; and
three of Noel Mooney's competitors, who had
ridden in from nearby townships especially for the
big Saturday night game. Mooney himself did not
participate. He was no gambling man and was
content to make his fortune without relying upon
the whims of Lady Luck.

Leney played as he lived. He was a bold,
sometimes audacious, yet never entirely reckless,

gambler. When the luck was with him, he would go for broke. When it wasn't, he was smart enough to draw in his horns a little. In consequence, as a winner, he was apt to win well; while, on the occasions he lost, his losses were invariably none too drastic.

On that particular Saturday night, Leney felt pretty darned confident, and his instincts did not let him down. The cards ran well for him. He had a number of very good hands, and he made the most of them. As a result, by the time the game ended at two o'clock the following morning, he was several hundred dollars ahead. Only James Higgins was also in profit, the rest having lost. Most had lost fairly heavily, although the banker, Fletcher Mulgrove, ever a canny player, had succeeded in limiting his losses to a little less than twenty dollars.

As the party split up, Higgins joined Leney at the bar for a final drink.

'Wa'al, Chuck,' said the mayor, 'you sure were in good form tonight!'

'Yeah, guess I was on quite a roll,' replied the rancher.

'You had the Devil's own luck.'

Chuck Leney grinned.

'I don't deny it,' he chuckled.

He glanced round the bar-room. All the other games had broken up sometime earlier. There were few drinkers left and the saloon girls had pretty well run out of customers. Only one of the five was upstairs, engaged in her professional duties. The rest were drinking and smoking at the far end of the bar-counter, patiently awaiting Noel Mooney's permission to retire for the night. Chuck Leney caught Bonnie Regan's eye and again smiled at the redhead.

His marriage had been one of convenience, at least as far as he was concerned. Anxious to have a son to succeed him, Leney had married the daughter of a neighbouring rancher, a girl twenty years his junior. At first, her youthful freshness had kept him faithful, but at the onset of her first pregnancy, Leney had reverted to his old dissolute bachelor ways and recommenced fornicating with, amongst others, Noel Mooney's sporting women. Most Saturday nights, once the poker game ended, the rancher would take one or other of the saloon girls to bed. His favourite, up to the present, had been a petite bottle-blonde with saucy eyes and an ability to please him that bordered on the miraculous. Tonight, however, he fancied sampling the charms of Mooney's latest acquisition, the red-haired Bonnie Regan.

Once James Higgins had finished his drink and departed through the batwing doors into the night, Leney placed his empty glass on the marbled bar-top and, with a flick of his forefinger, gestured to the redhead that she should join him. She glanced at Noel Mooney, who was standing behind the bar, busily polishing glasses. He nodded and gave her a sly wink.

Bonnie Regan stubbed out her cigarette and smiled back at the rancher.

'You go with him, yuh ain't gonna git no sleep 'tween now an' daybreak,' murmured the bottle-blonde, speaking from personal experience.

'Don't s'ppose I am,' replied Bonnie, with a grin. 'But, then, I ain't overly weary.'

Neither was she. Besides, she had been told that Chuck Leney was one of the richest men in Montana and was renowned for his generosity.

Leney watched the young woman sidle along the bar towards him. His eyes lit up with pleasure and eager anticipation. Beneath the tumble of golden-red locks was a pretty, plump face, dancing green eyes and a wide, sensuous mouth. His eyes travelled down to the smooth white shoulders and large, firm breasts peeping provocatively out of the low-cut bodice of her tight-fitting green velvet dress. The rancher smiled broadly.

'Let's you an' me go upstairs, an' have ourselves a li'l fun,' he growled.

'That's why I'm here,' replied Bonnie, promptly tucking her arm into his.

Then without more ado, they headed for the stairway that led to the upper floor of Mooney's Saloon.

A few seconds later, they were inside one of the

upstairs bedrooms. And the door had scarcely closed before Chuck Leney started divesting himself of his coat.

'I can hardly wait!' he declared.

'Me neither,' grinned the redhead. 'But, first, you'll have to help me outa this here dress.'

'My pleasure,' said Leney, and he hastily began unlacing the velvet gown.

Dawn was breaking as Chuck Leney stepped through the batwing doors and out into Main Street. He was in a particularly good humour. He had been lucky at cards and had followed the poker game with a night to remember, for Bonnie Regan had surpassed even the bottle-blonde in her sensuality and eagerness to please.

A keen wind whistled through Main Street and Chuck Leney shivered slightly. Having only moments earlier left Bonnie's warm bed, he was more sensitive than usual to the chill morning air. He buttoned up his heavy sheepskin coat and hurried across the street to the livery stables. There he rousted out the ostler and, a few minutes later, he was mounted on his roan and cantering eastward along Main Street on his way home. Two hours' ride would take him to the Triple L, where he would get his wife to cook him a hearty breakfast. The very thought of it whetted his appetite, and he began to regret not having asked Noel Mooney to rustle him up some bacon and eggs before he left town.

Leney could, of course, have turned the roan's head and ridden back into Great Falls, but, now that he was mounted, he determined to keep going. It might be the Sabbath, yet it was no day of rest for the rancher. There was work that needed to be done and, the sooner he reached the Triple L, the sooner he could attend to it. Leney urged the roan on along the trail, hunching up as he did so, for he was riding directly into the wind.

Three miles from Great Falls, Leney had to make a decision. He could continue eastward and circle round the low hills that rose up in front of him, or he could cut through to the ranch by way of Owl Pass. The latter route would take at least a couple of miles off his journey, but would prove the more difficult ride, for the pass twisted and turned like a corkscrew and was strewn with boulders and loose scree. On a warm morning, and with a full belly, Chuck Leney would probably have chosen the longer, less tricky route. However, cold and hungry as he was, he opted for the short ride through Owl Pass.

Immediately, the rancher had to reduce his speed, as the roan started to pick her way through the rocks that littered the floor of the pass. The deeper into Owl Pass he ventured, the narrower Leney found it. The rock faces rose up precipitously on either side of him and the trail twisted its way round one bend after another.

The ride required all of Leney's concentration, for he had no wish that the roan should stumble and fall. His eyes, therefore, were aimed down at the rocky trail he was following, and it was not until he was within a few yards of the fellow that he suddenly observed the lone horseman blocking his path.

The man was small and stockily built and clothed in buckskins, with a raccoon-skin hat and Indian-style mocassins on his feet. He was mounted on a small black racing pony, of the kind favoured by Indian braves, and he rode without a saddle in the manner of an Indian. Jet-black hair hung to his shoulders and his bronzed features were as though carved from granite. Blazing black eyes gleamed fiercely from beneath an angry brow, and these combined with a large hooked nose and an uncompromising jaw to give the man's visage a fearsome, almost Satanic look. Only the lack of paint prevented him from looking the epitome of a brave on the warpath. Yet he was not an Indian, at least not wholly. He was a half-breed, the product of an Irish-American trapper and mountain man and his Crow squaw.

Chuck Leney viewed the half-breed with a cautious eye, warily noting the Winchester in the man's saddleboot, the .45 calibre Colt Peacemaker in the holster tied down on his right thigh, the two knives tucked into his belt, the one designed for stabbing and the other for skinning buffaloes and other game, and finally the tall lance clutched in his left hand. But it was not the lance itself that bothered the rancher, rather it was the seven human scalps tied to it, brandished by the half-breed as though they were battle-honours.

The rancher scowled and dropped his hand on to the butt of his Remington revolver. He addressed the small, buckskin-clad half-breed in a rough, peremptory manner.

'Git outa my way!' he rasped.

The half-breed smiled, but there was no laughter in his eyes, which stared venomously at the big rancher.

'You know who I am?' he enquired softly.

'Oh yeah, I can guess who you are! That goddam lance gives you away,' replied Leney.

'It's still short of a scalp or two.'

'Is that so?'

'It is.'

'Wa'al, you ain't gonna git my scalp, you murderin' sonofabitch!'

'No?'

'No, dammit!'

As he spoke, Chuck Leney made to grab the Remington out of its holster. But he never had been much of a hand with a gun and, before it had even cleared leather, he found himself staring down the barrel of the half-breed's Colt Peacemaker.

'Drop that gun,' said the half-breed.

14

Leney hesitated, then reluctantly let the Remington fall back into its holster. He slowly raised his hands, glaring angrily at the little man as he did so.

'What d'yuh want with me?' he growled.

'I think you know.'

'You ... you aimin' to kill me?'

'An' take yore scalp.'

'I told yuh, you ain't gonna git ...'

'Stop me.'

For a second time, Leney dropped his hand on to the butt of the Remington. It was, he realized, a hopeless gesture, but he knew the half-breed proposed to kill him and he intended to die fighting. To his surprise, this time he succeeded in pulling the gun clear of the holster. He swiftly raised it, but, as he did so, the half-breed fired. The bullet struck Leney in the right shoulder and knocked him clean out of the saddle. He cried out and hit the ground with a resounding thud, the revolver flying from his grasp and landing several yards away in the middle of a patch of scree.

The half-breed smiled grimly and dismounted. Still clutching the Colt Peacemaker, he advanced upon the prostrate rancher. He thrust the lance head first into the ground, switched the gun from his right to his left hand, and then crouched down beside the rancher. He jabbed the muzzle of the revolver hard into Leney's chest in the region of his heart. Leney gasped with pain. His right arm hung limply at his side, while blood oozed out through the bullet-hole in his sheepskin coat. He stared in horror at the half-breed as the little man slowly, purposefully, drew the knife he used for skinning from his belt.

'No ... no, you cain't mean to ...' began Leney, but the other cut him short.

'Oh, I mean to, all right!' rasped the half-breed.

In an act of sheer desperation, Chuck Leney attempted to lever himself upright. Using his good left arm and ignoring the revolver jabbed into his chest, he heaved himself into a sitting position. The half-breed made no attempt to prevent him, but simply withdrew the gun a few inches and then smashed him across the face with the barrel. There was a crunch of bone as the metal made contact with Leney's nose. Leney screamed and fell back, blood pouring from the mashed remains of his nose. Immediately, the half-breed pounced on him, pinning him to the ground. Dropping the Colt back into its holster, he stretched out his left hand and grabbed hold of Leney's steel-grey hair. Thereupon, wielding the knife with his right hand, he began slicing away at the rancher's scalp.

Finally, the half-breed rose to his feet. Leney's screams died away and he peered up through pain-filled eyes. The half-breed stood before him brandishing a bloody swatch of hair. His, Leney's scalp was about to be added to the seven already attached to the half-breed's lance.

16

When he had finished tying the scalp on to the lance, the little man turned his attention to the wounded, quietly moaning rancher. Once again he approached Leney, his harsh, dark features remaining stern and impassive. His black eyes, however, flashed furiously and regarded the rancher with murderous intent. He pulled the Colt Peacemaker from its holster and took careful aim.

'Now yo're gonna die,' he snarled.

'For Chrissake!' cried Leney.

'I don't believe in yore God,' retorted the half-breed, and he squeezed the trigger.

The .45 calibre slug blasted a hole in Chuck Leney's forehead, mid-way between his eyes, and exited out of the back of his bloodied skull. His head fell back and he lay there, staring sightlessly up into the morning sky. The half-breed glared down at the dead rancher for a few moments. Then, he laughed, a harsh, humourless guffaw, and, replacing the revolver in its holster, stooped down and began to lift the dead man.

It was no easy task carrying the big rancher across to where his horse was standing, and then slinging him across the saddle. Leney must have weighed at least four stone more than his killer, yet the small, stocky half-breed had a strength and toughness that belied his size. He accomplished the task with remarkably little effort.

Thereupon, with Chuck Leney tied securely

across the saddle and, so, unlikely to fall off, the half-breed mounted his black pony and, leading the roan by the bridle, set off through the pass in the direction of the Triple L ranch.

He quickly reached the end of Owl Pass and cantered out on to the prairie. Then, without a second's hesitation, he headed towards Chuck Leney's headquarters, where stood the ranch-house, cook-house, bunkhouse, stables, outbuildings and corral.

There were two of Leney's hands working in the corral. They paused in their work to watch the half-breed ride up. Suddenly, as he approached them, he raised the lance and let loose a wild Crow war-cry. then, abandoning the roan and her gruesome burden, he turned the pony's head and galloped off, back in the direction from which he had come.

The two cowboys hesitated for a moment or two, before one of them yelled, 'Ain't that the boss's roan?'

'Yo're right!' cried the other, and the pair hurriedly climbed out of the corral and began running towards the stationary animal.

They could see from the corral that there was a body draped across the saddle of the roan. But it was not until they reached the horse that they were able to determine it was a dead body and, worst of all, the body of their employer.

'Holy cow!' exclaimed the first of the two

cowboys to examine Chuck Leney's mutilated corpse. 'I'll be darned if the sonofabitch ain't gone an' scalped him!'

The second cowboy turned his face away, the colour fading from his cheeks. He gagged.

'Injun Joe Brady. That's who done it,' he croaked, staring bleakly across the prairie at the fast-disappearing half-breed.

'Yeah. That's gotta be him. Who else?' muttered his companion.

'The question is, who's gonna break the news to Mrs Leney?'

'We'll git Chester to do that. He's foreman, after all.'

So saying, the first cowboy took hold of the roan's bridle and, averting his gaze, began to lead the horse and her late owner towards the ranch-house.

TWO

The funeral took place in Great Falls. It was a grand, if sombre, occasion, attended by a fair number of Montana's wealthiest and most influential citizens. Amongst those dignitaries, who had come to pay their respects to the late, lamented Chuck Leney, were Benjamin F. Potts, the Governor of the State of Montana, who had journeyed over from the state capital, Helena; Colonel Matthew MacBain and Major Neil Saunders from nearby Fort F.C. Smith; Senator John Caine and Congressmen Luke Williams and Jerry Bates; James Higgins, the mayor of Great Falls; Sheriff Bob Blake and US Marshal Tom Playfair; Leney's fellow poker-players; the saloon-keeper, Noel Mooney; and almost all of Montana's leading ranchers.

The cortège was led by the rancher's widow, Louise Leney, a diminutive figure clad from head to toe in black. She clung to the arm of her father, the rancher Burt Dyson, while, with her other hand, she grasped the small fist of her five-year-old son, Chuck Junior. Her other two children, four-year-old Roy and three-year-old Dorothy, remained at home at the ranch-house, being cared for by her mother.

Burt Dyson could still scarcely believe that his son-in-law was dead. Although he was a mere five years older than Leney, he had lacked the dead man's drive and vigour, and could easily have been taken to be a good fifteen years his senior. It had never occurred to him, therefore, that he would out-live Leney. But now his daughter was the richest widow in the entire state, and he had the onerous task of running both the Triple L and his own ranch. He prayed that she would marry again soon, for he did not much fancy the idea of running both ranches until Chuck Junior was of an age to take over. Burt Dyson was not a particularly ambitious man and felt that the running of his own, rather smaller ranch was as much as he could happily cope with.

Louise Leney had quickly fallen out of love with her husband. His neglectful and rather boorish behaviour had seen to that. A quiet, submissive young woman, she had pursued her wifely duties to the best of her ability and, to console herself for his lack of affection, had lavished her love upon her children. They had been, and still were, her pride and joy. Chuck Leney's sudden and terrible death had shocked and saddened her, but she would surely get over it. She trudged along, flanked by her father and her small son, her eyes downcast and her mind still numbed by the unexpectedness of the rancher's demise.

The actual burial took place in a small graveyard situated on the western fringe of the town. The Reverend Elmer Noakes conducted the service in suitably funereal tones, the coffin was lowered slowly into the grave, Louise and her son each threw a sprinkling of dirt, and it was over.

Immediately thereafter, the mourners took it in turns to express their condolences to the grieving widow and, once these formalities had been concluded, Burt Dyson helped her and the boy into a gig and drove them off in the direction of the Triple L. Relatives and close friends followed, while the rest of the crowd slowly dispersed.

Burt Dyson had invited all of the dignitaries back to the ranch but a number declined, for they were anxious to return to their various duties. The Governor, Sheriff Bob Blake and US Marshal Tom Playfair all intended catching the next train out of Great Falls bound for Helena, while Colonel MacBain and Major Saunders wanted to return to Fort F.C. Smith as soon as possible.

The others gathered at the ranch-house. Refreshments had been laid on, and Senator John Caine, who had accepted Dyson's invitation, soon found himself clutching a glass of whiskey and standing in a small group, consisting of the two congressmen, the town mayor, Noel Mooney and Dyson himself.

Caine was a slim, handsome man in his late forties. His thick black hair was lightly flecked with grey, and his rather dark, saturnine features boasted a neat, pencil-thin moustache. He was dressed in a black coat and trousers, wore a low-crowned black Stetson and, although of no more than average height, invariably dominated any company in which he found himself.

He regarded his neighbours with a cool, perceptive eye. They, too, were all dressed in sombre black. Congressman Luke Williams was a large, fat, ruddy-faced man, with a jovial, hail-fellow-well-met manner, while his fellow politician, Jerry Bates, was small and thin-faced, a little weasel of a man. Both James Higgins the mayor and Noel Mooney the saloonkeeper were tall, imposing-looking figures, the former clean-shaven and the latter endowed with whiskers and beard. And Burt Dyson, short and stocky, with lean, weatherbeaten features and his hair prematurely white, looked exactly what he was: a cattleman and a plainsman.

'Wa'al, this sure is a bad business,' commented Noel Mooney glumly.

'It certainly is!' averred Congressman Williams.

'I s'pose there's no doubt that Chuck was a victim of this here Injun Joe Brady?' said Bates.

'None,' declared Dyson and, eyeing the politician coldly, he asked, 'You know 'bout Injun Joe, do yuh?'

"Course. Seems like he's a livin' legend in these parts. Since the fall of '79, he's murdered an' scalped no fewer 'n seven white men, apparently all jest chosen at random.'

'Eight,' said Dyson. 'Chuck was his eighth victim.'

'But how can you be certain that this Injun Joe has killed 'em all?' enquired Bates.

"Cause he's made darned sure there was never any doubt,' said Higgins. 'In each an' every case, he rode up with his mutilated victim to within a hundred yards or so of witnesses, brandished his scalp-laden lance, screamed out some kinda war-cry, an' then turned an' fled.'

'He wants it to be known that he murdered all these folks?'

'Guess so.'

'But why in tarnation?'

'Because, Jerry,' said John Caine, 'the breed's gone plumb loco.'

'That ain't exactly a reason,' retorted the congressman.

'It's the only one yo're likely to git,' said Mooney. 'There's some fellers, who ain't right in the head, who court that kinda fame. They reckon it'll give 'em some form of immortality. Wa'al, mebbe it will.'

'That's right. Billy the Kid was one such,' said Congressman Luke Williams.

'As is John Wesley Hardin,' added James Higgins.

'An' it seems Injun Joe Brady is yet another,' said Caine.

'Wa'al, the Kid's dead an' Hardin's in jail, an', anyways, neither of them ever troubled us way up here in Montana. But Injun Joe Brady is still on the loose, an' all I can say is, it's 'bout time the authorities caught up with an' hanged the sonofa-bitch! Hell, what do we pay our taxes for?' cried Burt Dyson angrily.

'You said it!' averred Noel Mooney.

'Aw, that ain't strictly fair!' exclaimed Williams. 'We've been doin' our best. Ain't that so, John?'

Senator John Caine nodded gravely.

'We have,' he said. 'First, there was that posse of US marshals that spent three whole months scourin' the Little Belt Mountains lookin' for him. They never got near an' eventually gave up. Then I persuaded Colonel MacBain to despatch a troop of bluecoats. But they had no more success than the marshals.'

Burt Dyson laughed harshly. 'An', so, you went an' gave up!' he rasped.

'There was that trio of bounty hunters, who ...'

'They wasn't official. They went on their own account, for the bounty.'

'That's true.'

'An' they never got near the murderin' sonofa-bitch neither.'

'No.'

'That was eight months back, Senator.'

26

'The winter ain't a good time to go off up into the mountains.'

'The winter don't seem to bother Injun Joe none.'

'He's a mountain man. Remember he's half Crow. What's Hell on earth to the likes of you an' me is plain home to him.'

'Wa'al, it's Spring now, an' most of the snows have gone off the mountains.'

'Yeah, that's right. An' Injun Joe's started killin' again. Somethin's gotta be done to prevent him attachin' any more scalps to that darned lance of his,' commented Mooney.

'I reckon it's up to the governor to take measures an' ...' began Luke Williams.

'You an' Jerry represent us congressmen, John's in the Senate an' James is mayor of Great Falls. Yo're all politicians who rely on our votes to keep you in office. Wa'al, if'n' yuh aim to keep our votes, I guess you'd better start doin' somethin' to earn 'em. The takin' of Injun Joe Brady is as much yore responsibility as it is Governor Potts',' declared Dyson.

'I agree with Burt. So, whaddya intend doin' 'bout it?' enquired Noel Mooney.

Luke Williams and Jerry Bates both looked worried men, while James Higgins coughed nervously and dropped his gaze. They had no answer. John Caine, on the other hand, remained his usual imperturbable self.

'I figure I've taken my responsibilities in this matter pretty darned seriously,' he said coolly.

'Oh, yeah?' growled the rancher.

'Yeah. Who was it that induced the governor to send them US marshals into the mountains after the 'breed?' he demanded.

'You, Senator?'

'Yup. An' as I've already told you, when they failed to catch him, I persuaded Colonel MacBain to despatch a troop of soldiers in search of him.'

'They also failed to catch him.'

'We've already established that, Burt.'

'So?'

'So, this time, I swear I'll git him.'

'This time?'

'There's a reward for Injun Joe's capture dead or alive. Five thousand dollars is the price on his head. Wa'al, I'm aimin' to recruit me a bunch of bounty hunters by promisin' to double that reward.'

James Higgins whistled softly, while the others stared in amazement at the senator.

'That's one helluva sum to come outa yore own pocket, John!' commented Jerry Bates.

'Yeah. But, y'see, it's gotten kinda personal 'tween me an' the 'breed.'

'Whaddya mean?' asked Dyson.

'I knew all of the men he's killed, some better'n others. The banker, Andrew Smith, for instance, was best man at my weddin' an' godfather to my daughter, Kitty.'

'You want revenge; it's as simple as that,' said Mooney.

'Yo're darn tootin' I do! Both Andrew Smith an' Injun Joe's third victim, Bill Lloyd, were real good friends of mine since boyhood days. I cain't jest sit back an' do nuthin',' said the senator vehemently.

'So, yo're invitin' these bounty hunters to form a … a kinda posse to go after the 'breed?' said Dyson.

'That's right, Burt. An' I aim to lead it myself.'

'How many bounty hunters are yuh figurin' on takin' along?' enquired Higgins.

'Ten, an' a scout to guide us an' pick up Injun Joe's trail.'

'Whew! You sure do mean business. That's one helluva lotta gunslingers to hunt down jest the one feller,' remarked Mooney.

'Wa'al, Injun Joe ain't no ordinary feller.'

'You can say that again!' exclaimed Luke Williams. 'The murderin' sonofabitch may be plumb loco, but he's sure provin' a difficult man to catch!'

'As elusive an' as deadly as a goddam copperhead,' added Jerry Bates.

'One thing's for certain,' said Higgins. 'Jim Bell won't be none too happy 'bout a bunch of bounty hunters stoppin' over in Great Falls.'

John Caine nodded. He knew what the mayor said what true. Marshal Jim Bell was the kind of

lawman who preferred to forestall trouble
wherever and whenever possible. Bell kept a
sharp eye on every stranger who rode into Great
Falls and, if he suspected someone was likely to
cause trouble, he had no compunction in ordering
that man to mosey on out of town. He wanted
nothing more than a quiet town and a quiet life,
and he made darned sure that that was what he
got. It was certain, therefore, that Jim Bell would
not welcome the arrival of several gunslingers.

'The marshal will jest have to tolerate their
presence,' commented the senator.

'Wa'al, I jest pray they don't cause no trouble
while they're in town,' said Higgins. 'I don't s'pose
they'll be long in Great Falls?' he murmured
hopefully.

'Only for as long as it takes 'em all to git here,'
said Caine. 'Once all ten are gathered together, I'll
pick up a scout an' we'll set out at once for the
Little Belt Mountains.'

'You got a scout in mind?' enquired Dyson.

'Yeah. Red Knife.'

'You sure? Remember, Red Knife's a Crow.'

'So?'

'Brady is half Crow.'

'Don't worry, Burt. I reckon I can persuade Red
Knife to come along,' said Caine.

'Wa'al, he sure is one helluva good scout. Let's
hope the bounty hunters you've chosen are half as
good at their trade as he is at his,' said Mooney.

'Oh, you can be sure they are! I've picked them by reputation.'

This was true. Caine had taken advice from both US Marshal Tom Playfair and Sheriff Bob Blake, and they had given him the names of men who had survived several years in their dangerous profession.

'When are you expectin' them all to arrive in Great Falls?' enquired Noel Mooney.

'Dunno exactly. There's two up here in Montana, while the rest are scattered far an' wide. I telegraphed 'em to git here jest as soon as they can, an' I guess that's what they'll do,' replied Caine.

'Yo're gonna wait till they git here an' then take off with them into the mountains?' said Jerry Bates.

'That's what I said,' stated Caine.

'But that means yo're gonna miss one helluva lot of senate business,' remarked the little congressman.

'That's too bad, but I gotta see this thing through. I owe it to my dear departed friends an' to the people of this here state. While Injun Joe Brady remains a livin' legend, they're all gonna be in fear of their lives. Hell, nobody knows when or where that murderin' maniac is likely to strike next.'

'Well spoken, Senator. I'm glad to see yo're takin' yore obligations so seriously,' said Neil Mooney.

'Me, too,' averred Burt Dyson.

'It ain't that Jerry an' me don't wanta …' began

Luke Williams anxiously, but he was cut short by Caine.

'It's OK, boys,' said the senator genially. ''Course I know you'd both be willin' to play a part in bringin' Injun Joe to justice. It's jest that I got in first an', 'sides, like I said, I got more reason to take an active role, what with Andrew Smith an' Bill Lloyd bein' such old an' dear friends of mine.'

He finished his whiskey and glanced round for somewhere to place the glass. As he did so, Burt Dyson stepped forward and took it from his hand.

'Can I git you another?' he asked.

'No thanks, Burt. Reckon I'll be goin'. Thanks for yore hospitality, an' you take good care of Louise now.'

'I will. You may depend on that.' Burt Dyson smiled grimly, and the two men shook hands. 'Good luck!' he said. 'May you soon catch up with that bastard. An' when yuh do....'

'I'll bring you his scalp,' Caine promised the rancher.

THREE

Four days had elapsed since the funeral of Chuck Leney when a stranger rode into the frontier town of Great Falls. He was a tall, broad-shouldered Kentuckian, mounted on a bay gelding. He wore a grey Stetson, a red kerchief round his neck, a knee-length buckskin jacket, grey shirt and faded blue denim pants. Pale-blue eyes peered out from a rugged, square-cut face. Grey-flecked brown hair, a multitude of lines around his eyes and a once-broken nose tended to make him look rather older than his thirty-odd years. He had lived a full and dangerous life and these days was looking for a little peace and quiet.

The Kentuckian dismounted in front of Mooney's Saloon and tied the gelding to the hitching-rail. Then, he turned and made as though to climb the short flight of wooden steps from the street to the stoop outside the saloon. As he did so, the batwing doors were thrown open and two men stepped out on to the stoop.

They were a disparate pair. Moose Donovan was a huge mountain of a man, while his companion, Eddie Winn, was of no more than average height and as thin as a rake.

Neither man wore a coat for, in the four days since the funeral, the wind had changed direction and dropped considerably and, as a result, the temperature had risen sharply. Spring had finally arrived.

Moose Donovan wore a battered brown Stetson and a brown leather vest over a threadbare check shirt. Like the Kentuckian, he sported a pair of faded blue denim pants and unspurred leather boots. Eddie Winn was similarly clad, although, in place of Donovan's Stetson, he wore a brown Derby hat. Both men were unshaven and menacing-looking, Donovan resembling an irate grizzly and Winn a particularly mean and vicious coyote. Yet, despite their frightening aspects, neither man carried a gun.

Moose Donovan glanced down at the approaching Kentuckian, gasped with surprise and came to an abrupt halt.

'Holy cow, if it ain't Jack Stone the famous lawman!' he sneered.

'I ain't a lawman no more,' replied the Kentuckian evenly.

'No? Got tired of shootin' folks?' enquired Donovan sarcastically.

'Something like that,' said Stone.

Donovan turned to his thin-faced companion.

'Stone here's the bastard who shot my cousin, Sam, back in Pocatello, Idaho,' he explained.

'I did so only in the line of duty,' said Stone.

'In the line of duty! Huh!'

'It was him or me, Moose.'

'Wa'al, I don't take none too kindly to fellers who kill my kin.'

'Don't s'pose you do. But that was 'bout seven years back. Surely you ain't still harbourin' a grudge?'

'I've got a long memory, an' I do tend to bear grudges.'

'So, whaddya propose doin? I see you ain't wearin' no gun.'

Donovan and his companion exchanged glances. then, Donovan glared at Stone and snarled, 'I don't need no gun to avenge Sam's death.'

'No?' said the Kentuckian.

'Nope. I reckon to tear you apart with my bare hands.'

'You tell him, Moose!' cried Winn, his coal-black eyes glistening with venom, and he added scornfully, 'I don't b'lieve the sonofabitch has the guts to face up to you, not without that there Frontier Model Colt to protect him.'

'Keep outa this, feller,' rasped Stone. 'This matter is 'tween me an' Moose.'

'Take off yore gun-belt then, an' let's see what kinda man you really are!' growled Donovan.

Jack Stone hesitated. He did his best these days
to avoid trouble, and he certainly had no wish to
fight Moose Donovan. On the other hand, his
pride would not let him walk away from the man's
challenge. He tried one last time to sue for peace.

'Aw, come on, Moose!' he said. 'Let's forget the
past an' go have a drink together.'

Moose Donovan shook his huge, shaggy head
and stood there, barring the Kentuckian's passage
with his immense bulk.

'You wanta drink in this here saloon, Stone,' he
said belligerently, 'then you gotta settle with me
first.'

So saying, he handed Eddie Winn his hat and
vest. Stone shrugged his brawny shoulders. By
now a small crowd had gathered. He handed his
Stetson and his buckskin jacket to a little,
bespectacled clerk from the general store across
the street. His gun-belt and his Frontier Model
Colt he gave to a large, florid-faced, prosperous-
looking gent in a smart city-style suit, a gent
whom he reckoned would be unlikely to run off
with them. In this calculation Stone was quite
right, for the prosperous-looking gent was none
other than Fletcher Mulgrove, the banker, one of
Great Falls' most respectable citizens.

The two protagonists stepped into the middle of
the street and the crowd, which was increasing by
the minute, formed a rough circle round them.

'Go git him, Moose!' yelled Eddie Winn.

The big man needed no second urging. He lunged at the Kentuckian and let fly with a wild haymaker. Stone easily ducked beneath it and countered by jabbing his right hand into the other's face: once, twice, thrice. Stone was no man mountain like his opponent, yet he, too, was a big man and he carried a hefty punch. Consequently, the three punches did Moose Donovan no little damage. His lower lip was split open, three teeth were loosened and his nose was broken and streaming with blood.

Howling with rage and pain, Donovan charged blindly at the Kentuckian, throwing punches as he came. Again Stone easily dodged the other's wild, cumbersome swings and hit him hard in the belly. Donovan gasped and, as his jaw fell open, Stone caught him a vicious right uppercut. The force of the blow lifted Donovan clean off his feet and he landed on his back in the dust with a tremendous, earth-shattering thud.

He lay there for some moments, his face masked with blood and his brains scrambled. Slowly, painfully, he staggered to his feet and shook his head. His brain began to clear and he glared furiously at the Kentuckian.

'I'll git you, yuh bastard!' he snarled, and once more he charged like a berserk grizzly towards his tormentor.

Stone hit Donovan hard on the temple with a sledgehammer blow, but this time did not succeed in halting Donovan's charge. The giant caught hold of the Kentuckian in a bear-like hug and began to squeeze. Stone gasped as Donovan piled on the pressure. He felt as though his ribs were about to cave in. He struggled to break the other's vice-like grip, but to no avail. Then, in desperation, he brought up his right knee and drove it into Donovan's groin. Donovan hollered and fell back, clutching at his private parts. As he did so, Stone drew back his right fist and smashed it into his opponent's bloodied, broken nose with all the force he could muster. The scream of pain that rent the air could easily have been heard at the far end of town.

Moose Donovan dropped on to one knee and held up his hand. He had had enough. A big bully of a man, he was used to inflicting pain, yet quite unaccustomed to receiving it. And the thought of taking another blow to his badly damaged nose simply terrified him.

His capitulation did not, however, go down too well with his companion.

'You surely ain't gonna quit, are yuh, Moose?' yelled Eddie Winn, as he shot a venomous glance at Stone.

Moose Donovan made no response. He remained on one knee, his head bowed and dripping blood. He was beaten and he knew it.

'Yore pardner ain't as dumb as he looks. He knows when he's beat,' said Stone and, turning his back on the battered, bleeding giant, he stepped across and took the buckskin jacket from the little, bespectacled clerk.

It was as Stone went to retrieve his gun from Fletcher Mulgrove that Eddie Winn made his move. Stooping down, he pulled up his trouser-leg and whipped a knife from out of his boot. He darted past the still bemused Moose Donovan and towards the unsuspecting Kentuckian. He was a mere yard away when a voice behind him caused him to halt.

'Drop that knife or I'll blow yore goddam head off!'

Winn straightway froze and slowly, reluctantly, lowered the knife. Then he let it fall to the ground. He half-turned and found himself facing the town marshal. Jim Bell was a slim, dapper figure in a grey city suit and grey Derby hat. He had a frank, rather boyish countenance and looked more like a bank clerk than a lawman. But one glance into Bell's steely grey eyes confirmed that he was much tougher than he looked. He was quite prepared to kill anyone who threatened the peace, a fact which was not lost upon Eddie Winn, as he stared nervously into the muzzle of the marshal's Colt Peacemaker.

'I knew it was a mistake to let you darned bounty hunters stay over in Great Falls,' rasped Bell. 'Even when yo're forbidden to carry guns within the town limits, yuh still git into trouble.'

He turned and fixed Stone with a baleful stare. 'I s'pose yo're the latest of Senator Caine's recruits to hit town?' he said.

'I don't know no Senator Caine,' replied Stone.

'Then, you ain't one of the bounty hunters he's hired to go after Injun Joe Brady?' said Bell.

'No, Marshal, I ain't. I'm jest passin' through yore town, on my way north to do a li'l huntin'.'

'So, how come you got into a fight with Donovan?' enquired the marshal.

'That's what I'd like to know,' said Senator John Caine, as he pushed his way through the crowd to confront Stone and the two bounty hunters.

'Ah, Senator!' Jim Bell greeted the newcomer with a grim smile. 'Seems yore boys jest cain't keep outa trouble.'

'Wa'al, we don't know yet what caused the fight, Marshal. Mebbe Moose....'

'Yore hired gun nurses a grudge,' said Stone. 'I shot an' killed his cousin 'bout seven years back in Pocatello, Idaho. I was deputy US marshal at the time, an' Moose's cousin was ridin' with a bunch of no-account bank robbers.'

'You say you was a lawman!' exclaimed Bell. 'Wa'al, why d'yuh quit? Huh?'

'Guess I got tired of puttin' my life on the line. I reckon to take things easy these days.'

'You got a name, mister?'

'Stone. Jack Stone.'

Both Marshal Jim Bell and Senator John Caine

glanced at each other, then turned again to face the Kentuckian.

'The same Jack Stone who helped Bat Masterson clean up Dodge City?' asked the marshal.

'The feller who's known throughout the West as the man who tamed Mallory?' enquired the senator.

'That's me.'

'You got one helluva reputation, Mr Stone,' remarked Bell.

'You sure have,' said Caine. 'An' I'm real sorry 'bout this whole shindig.' He glared at Moose Donovan, who, by this time, had staggered to his feet. 'You ain't here in Great Falls to settle old scores, Moose,' he snapped. 'Yo're here at my expense as part of the posse I'm formin' to go after Injun Joe Brady. So, you an' Eddie stay away from Mr Stone from now on, an' keep outa trouble. You hear me?'

'Yeah. Sorry, Mr Caine,' mumbled Donovan.

'You best go git cleaned up,' said the senator, and, as the pair made to slink off, he held out his hand. 'Gimme that knife, Eddie,' he rasped.

Eddie Winn bent down and picked up the weapon. He glared malevolently at the Kentuckian, but did as he was bid and handed the knife to Caine. Then, he and Donovan headed back towards their hotel, where the injured giant intended to clean up his face and place a cold compress on his badly smashed nose. As they departed, Marshal Jim Bell turned and faced Caine.

'I told you to keep those lunkheads outa trouble, Senator,' he said angrily.

'I know, Marshal, an' I apologize. But it was jest unlucky that Moose should go an' bump into the feller who shot his cousin. There won't be no more trouble, I promise you.'

'Wa'al, the sooner the rest of yore hired guns arrive an' you all set out after Injun Joe, the better,' commented Bell.

'They should all be on their way by now. I figure the last of 'em will have gotten here by the end of this week at the very latest.'

'I sure hope so, for I don't like that kinda trash in my town.'

'Hell, Marshal, I know you ain't got no great likin' for bounty hunters! But I believe, in the present circumstances, they're a necessary evil. Neither the law nor the army have been able to catch up with Injun Joe, an' you ain't about to go after him, now are yuh?'

'I've got a duty to keep the peace here in Great Falls. I cain't go ridin' off into the mountains in pursuit of that mad, murderin' half-breed.'

'I know you cain't. Which is why I'm askin' yuh to exercise a li'l tolerance regardin' the presence of a few bounty hunters here in town.'

'If 'n' they cause no trouble, I'll exercise that tolerance. Otherwise....' Marshal Jim Bell left the rest unsaid.

He turned abruptly on his heel and headed back

towards his law office. John Caine frowned, and then shrugged his shoulders and directed his attention to the Kentuckian.

'Senator John Caine at yore service, Mr Stone,' he said, extending his hand. 'By way of reparation, let me buy you a drink.'

'Aw, it wasn't none of yore fault, Senator,' drawled Stone. 'Still, I'll take you up on that offer with pleasure.'

The two men shook hands and then, climbing up on to the stoop, they pushed open the batwing doors and entered Mooney's Saloon. They made their way across the bar-room to the marble-topped counter, where Caine asked for a bottle of whiskey and two glasses. He poured a couple of stiff whiskies and, raising his glass, remarked, 'Yore good health, Mr Stone.'

'An' yore's, Senator,' responded the Kentuckian.

Both men emptied their glasses at one draught, whereupon the senator promptly replenished them.

'You've heard of this Injun Joe Brady?' he growled.

Stone nodded.

'Yeah. He's some kinda legend in these parts.'

'He certainly is. He's gotten folks terrorized across the length an' breadth of the entire State of Montana.'

'How many fellers has he murdered so far?'

'Eight.'

'All random killin's?'

'Yup.'

'There ain't no rhyme nor reason to these killin's?'

'None that I can make out. Seems he's gone stark, starin' mad. Where you or I might git our fun outa sleepin' with a pretty woman, Injun Joe seems to git his from killin' an' scalpin' white folks.'

'I see.' Stone sipped his whiskey and commented quietly. 'You appear to be takin' a real personal interest in bringin' him to justice.'

'Sure am,' agreed Caine. 'I owe it to my constituents an', 'sides, I knew all of Injun Joe's victims.'

'So they was friends of yourn?'

'Not exactly. Most were merely acquaintances. But two were certainly friends, very close friends of mine. An' his latest victim, the rancher Chuck Leney, played a big part in gittin' me elected to the senate.'

'Which is why yo're gatherin' together a gang of bounty hunters to track him down?'

'Yup.'

'How many have you sent for?'

'Ten.'

'That's one helluva lot of hired guns to go after jest one lone killer.'

'Noel over there made that same remark,' said Caine, indicating the saloonkeeper, who was standing at the far side of the bar, smoking a large cigar. 'But, as I told him, Injun Joe Brady ain't no ordinary killer.'

'No, I guess not.'

'You wouldn't consider puttin' off yore huntin' trip for a while, would yuh, Mr Stone?'

'What, an' join yore expedition?'

'That's right. We sure could use a gunfighter of yore proven calibre.'

'Moose Donovan an' his pal might not like the idea of me ridin' along.'

'I decide who rides in this posse. Donovan an' Winn ain't got no say in the matter. Wa'al, whaddya say?'

'I was a lawman once.'

'So?'

'So, Senator, I have the same dislike of bounty hunters that yore marshal has. A law-officer shootin' an outlaw in the course of his duty's one thing; a private citizen huntin' that outlaw down for the price on his head is somethin' else.'

'Anyone who hunts down Injun Joe Brady is doin' society a favour. The 'breed's an evil, murderin' savage who has struck fear into the hearts of jest about every livin' soul hereabouts.'

'Wa'al, I'm afraid I cain't oblige you, Senator.'

'Won't oblige me.'

'Put it any way you like.'

'If 'n' you won't hunt Injun Joe for the price on his head, hows 'bout actin' as guide at a set wage of, say, ten dollars a day?'

'You want me to scout for you?'

'That's right. I b'lieve you was an Army scout once, an' a pretty darned good 'un?'

'Yeah. I gave up 'cause I couldn't stomach what the bluecoats was doin' to the Injuns.'

'Wa'al, all you'll be doin' this time is help track down the half-breed murderer of eight honest, Godfearin' white men. Surely you cain't object to that?'

Stone smiled thinly.

'I dunno,' he said.

'I was thinkin' of hirin' a Crow off the reservation, a brave called Red Knife, but I'd much sooner have you scout for us. It'll be kinda intriguin', one livin' legend stalkin' another.'

'Hmm....'

'Think it over, Mr Stone. If 'n' it's more money you want ...?'

'No. Ten dollars a day is jest fine. Mighty generous in fact. But I still ain't sure I want the job.'

'However, you'll think it over?'

'Yeah, Senator, I'll think it over.'

'Good!' John Caine smiled his most expansive smile and finished his second whiskey. Then, he placed the empty glass on the counter and remarked, 'I got things to do, Mr Stone, but I'll be around. So, jest let me know when you make up yore mind.' He glanced across towards Noel

Mooney and said, 'This here bottle's paid for, Noel. You put it on my tab, OK?'

In the event, Jack Stone finished his second whiskey and poured himself just once more, before pushing the bottle back across the counter to the saloonkeeper. He had some thinking to do, and he did not want his deliberations influenced by a large intake of alcohol.

By the time he had emptied the third glass, Stone knew exactly what he needed to do next. He ambled out of the saloon and made his way slowly and deliberately along the sidewalk to the law office, where he found Jim Bell sitting at his desk, contentedly smoking a cheroot and drinking coffee.

FOUR

Jack Stone drew up a chair opposite the marshal, pulled a cheroot from the pocket of his buckskin jacket and proceeded to light it.

'Coffee, Mr Stone?' enquired the lawman hospitably.

'Don't mind if I do,' replied Stone.

Once the marshal had poured Stone's coffee and the two men were sitting comfortably, facing each other, he said, 'Wa'al, Mr Stone, what can I do for you?'

'I wanta know a li'l more 'bout this Injun Joe Brady,' replied the Kentuckian.

'How much d'yuh know already?' asked Jim Bell.

'Only that he's a half-breed who's gone loco an' murdered an' scalped eight white folks, all seemin'ly chosen at random.'

'That's 'bout all there is to know.'

'When did these killin's begin?'

'Approximately three years ago. The first victim

49

was a rancher called Jake Richards. Then, a few months later, Injun Joe killed an' scalped Walter Flannery, the mayor of Lewistown.'

'An' since then he has killed an' scalped a further six fellers, includin' two close friends of Senator John Caine?'

'That's right. His last victim was Chuck Leney, whose Triple L ranch is only a few miles to the east of Great Falls. Injun Joe bushwhacked him on the way back from his reg'lar Saturday night poker game here in town.' Bell blew out a thin stream of tobacco-smoke and added grimly, 'In case yo're wonderin', there's no doubt Injun Joe was the killer in each an' every case.'

'No?'

'No. He always makes darned sure there ain't no doubt. Shows himself. Seems to want folks to know he's the killer.'

'That's kinda crazy.'

'Sure is. But, then, shootin' an' scalpin' ain't exactly the act of someone in his right mind.'

'No, I guess not.' Stone stared the marshal straight in the eye and asked, 'Any idea why he started killin'? Did somethin' happen three years ago to send him crazy?'

'I can only assume it was the death of his wife that did it.'

'Tell me about that.'

'Wa'al, Injun Joe Brady was the result of a union 'tween an Irish-American trapper an' an

Injun squaw. His mother was a Crow an', when Injun Joe took it into his head to marry, he followed his father's example an' also married a Crow girl. A pretty li'l thing by all accounts. Not that I ever saw her. Injun Joe was a loner, y'see, an' scarcely ever came into town 'cept to sell his skins. He an' the girl lived Injun-style in a tepee, way up in the Little Belt Mountains.'

'So, at the time of his marriage, he was regarded as a harmless kinda feller?'

'Yeah. Like I said, he wasn't much in town. But, certainly, he never caused no trouble when he did ride in. A peaceable character, quiet an' self-contained.'

'An' then his wife died. How did that happen?'

'I dunno for sure. Rumour is she died in childbirth, with the child stillborn.'

'Jeez! That's enough to send any man a li'l crazy.' Stone spoke from experience, for, some years previously, his young wife had died in similar circumstances, with the child stillborn. He had taken to the bottle, and it was some months before he had recovered. By then he had become a changed man, one who would always be moving on, always looking for another frontier to cross. He smiled bleakly as he added, 'I'm surprised, though, that it turned somebody, who you described as quiet, self-contained an' peaceable, into a cold-blooded killer.'

'That's human bein's for yuh, Mr Stone. Unpredictable.'

'Yeah.'

'So, what's yore interest?'

'Senator Caine wants me to act as guide on his expedition up into the Little Belt Mountains.'

'You gonna oblige him?'

'I ain't sure. I cain't say I fancy ridin' with bounty hunters.'

'I'm with you there,' said Bell. 'My main concern is that those sonsofbitches don't start shootin' up Great Falls. I want 'em in an' outa town as soon as possible.'

'Yeah. Wa'al, I guess I'll wait to see who's ridin' with the senator 'fore I commit myself.'

'That seems reasonable.'

'I'm surprised the senator is proposin' to go along.'

'He's taken the killin's kinda personal.'

'Even so, trackin' a notorious killer through mountain terrain ain't somethin' I'd recommend for a feller used to city life.'

'Oh, John Caine ain't entirely a stranger to the Little Belt Mountains! 'Deed, last time he rode up into the mountains, it was for pleasure,' reminisced the marshal.

'When was that?' asked Stone.

'In the fall of '79, as I recall. He had jest got hisself elected to the Senate an' Great Falls was crammed full of his supporters. By way of celebration, he took a bunch of 'em off on a huntin' trip. They was gone 'bout a week. Came back laden with trophies of the hunt: elks' heads, bear-skins, that kinda thing.'

'Who, besides Senator Caine, made up the huntin' party?'

'I don't rightly remember. There was so many strangers in town to celebrate his election victory.'

'You don't remember anyone who was part of that expedition?'

Marshal Jim Bell thought hard. Very hard. It was some minutes before his mind cleared, and he was able to inform the Kentuckian, 'Oh, yeah, now I come to think of it, Chuck Leney was one of Caine's party. He was, I believe, the only feller to go from round these parts.'

Stone nodded.

'That's interestin',' he said. 'Can you recall whether Caine an' his pals went off on their huntin' trip before or after the death of Injun Joe Brady's wife?'

Bell frowned.

'What are you implyin'?' he asked curiously.

'Dunno exactly. Wa'al …?'

'I honestly cain't remember.'

'So, who would know?'

'I ain't sure that anyone's likely to remember exactly when Injun Joe's wife died.'

'Where was she buried?'

'On the Crow reservation. Come to think of it, I s'pose the Injuns would remember. You could ride out there an' ask.'

Stone comtemplated this course of action, but decided against taking it, at least for the present.

"Fore I do that, I'd like to know the make-up of Caine's huntin' party,' he said.

'Wa'al, you could ask the senator,' suggested Bell.

Stone shook his head. He had only the vaguest of suspicions, but, should it prove to be correct, then the senator was the last man he ought to approach.

'I'd rather not,' he said. 'Who else'd know?'

'Jean-Pierre Lapointe, I s'pose.'

'Who's he?'

'A French-Canadian trapper. He acted as their guide.'

'An' jest where would I find this Lapointe feller?'

'That's a good question.'

'Whaddya mean?'

'Wa'al, y'see,' drawled Bell, 'Jean-Pierre never returned to Great Falls. Seems he made up his mind to head back across the border to Canada. An' once he'd seen the huntin' party safely on their way home, he did jest that.'

'Upped an' left 'em?'

'You got it, Mr Stone.'

The Kentuckian frowned.

'A kinda sudden decision, surely?' he commented.

'Yup. Guess he got homesick or somethin'.'

'Hmm.' Stone eyed the marshal coolly and then

enquired, 'Have you any idea whereabouts in Canada he was headed for?'

'Dunno for sure. Why d'yuh ask?'

'I'd like to speak to him.'

''Bout Caine's huntin' party?'

'Yup.'

'You *do* think there's a connection 'tween that an' the death of Injun Joe's wife, don't yuh, Mr Stone?'

'I think there's a distinct possibility, Marshal. You said that Chuck Leney was a member of that there huntin' party. S'pose the rest of Injun Joe's victims were too; s'pose they weren't simply random killin's? You sure yuh cain't recall who else Caine invited along?'

'No I cain't remember. Hell, I didn't know none of Injun Joe's other victims personally! Chuck Leney was the only one I was acquainted with. The rest were jest names to me. Whether they was members of that huntin' party, wa'al, I'm afraid I jest don't know.'

'So, Jean-Pierre Lapointe is the feller I gotta talk to. You said you didn't know for certain whereabouts in Canada he was headed. Could you hazard a guess?'

'Jean-Pierre often spoke of a sister livin' in Medicine Hat. That's way up beyond the Milk River.'

'Right.'

'You figurin' on ridin' up there to see if 'n' you

can find him?'

'Mebbe.'

'Medicine Hat must be a good hundred an' fifty miles north of here.'

'Yeah.'

'That's surely one helluva long ride jest to satisfy yore curiosity, Mr Stone?'

Stone nodded. Marshal Jim Bell was right. It was a long ride. But it was not merely a question of satisfying his curiosity. Stone felt a tremendous empathy towards the half-breed. They had each suffered a similar tragedy and all the grief and anguish that naturally followed. He could appreciate the awful torments Injun Joe Brady must have endured. He could so easily put himself in the other's place, and his heart went out to the man. That Injun Joe's killings were linked to the death of his wife, there seemed little doubt. But were they simply the random actions of a deranged mind? Stone's instincts told him that they were not, and his instincts rarely let him down. Therefore, because he felt Injun Joe to be a kindred spirit, the Kentuckian determined to get to the truth of the matter. He could do no other.

'I gotta find out the truth,' he growled.

'In that case, you won't be scoutin' for Senator Caine, when he an' his band of bounty hunters set off on Injun Joe's trail?' said Bell.

'No, Marshal, I won't. An' I'd appreciate it if 'n' you'll keep our li'l conversation to yoreself,' said

Stone.

'You don't want Senator Caine to know yo're diggin' into the past, huh?'

'That's 'bout it. If it turns out there ain't no connection 'tween his huntin' party an' Injun Joe suddenly takin' to scalpin' an' killin' white folks, that'll be an end to the matter as far as I'm concerned.'

'An' if 'n' there is a connection?'

'It depends what that connection is.'

'Wa'al, good luck, anyway, Mr Stone.'

'Thanks, Marshal.'

Jim Bell watched the big Kentuckian leave the law office and head off up Main Street in the direction of Mooney's Saloon where he had left his bay gelding tied to the hitching-post. The marshal mulled over what Stone had said. He had never before suspected that there was a link between Senator John Caine's expedition into the Little Belt Mountains and the death of Injun Joe Brady's pregnant squaw. That her death had occurred in the year 1879, the year Caine was elected to the senate, was not in dispute. He wished he could recall just when in that year she had died.

Jack Stone, meantime, had reached the saloon and mounted his horse. He wanted to speak with Jean-Pierre Lapointe as soon as possible. If his vague suspicions proved to be correct, time was of the essence. He smiled grimly to himself. He had given up his profession as a lawman in favour of a quiet life, and yet here he was, proposing to involve himself in something which was none of his business and could, ultimately, prove to be extremely dangerous indeed!

He turned the gelding's head and cantered off along Main Street. It was late afternoon and the frame buildings cast long shadows across the street. There were few people about. Stone glanced negligently to his left. As he did so, his keen eye chanced to catch sight of a sudden glint. A thin shaft of sunlight had split the shadows and struck something metallic. The barrel of a gun! Stone was leaping from the saddle as the revolver barked. In consequence, the shot whistled harmlessly over his head. He hit the dirt and dived head first behind a nearby water-trough. Stone's would-be assassin's second shot stirred up a spurt of dust inches away from his face, while the bushwhacker's third shot slammed into the side of the trough.

By this time, Stone had pulled his Frontier Model Colt free from its holster. The Kentuckian peered cautiously round the corner of the trough. Simultaneously, another bullet thudded into its side, missing him by a whisker. But this shot had been fired from behind him!

Stone whirled round to confront the second bushwhacker, and there, running towards him from his hiding-place deep in the shadows of an alleyway, was the huge, lumbering figure of Moose Donovan. The bounty hunter's ugly, unshaven face was contorted into an angry scowl and he was toting a Remington in his right hand. As he ran, he fired, but shooting on the run does not make for accuracy and, anyway, Moose Donovan was no great shot. He and Eddie Winn had, between them, hunted down and shot a number of dangerous outlaws in their time. However, on each and every occasion, they had relied upon an ambush and a shot in the back. This time their ambush had gone disastrously wrong.

Jack Stone aimed and fired the Colt in one swift, fluent movement. Twice he squeezed the trigger and split-seconds later a couple of .45 calibre slugs exploded into the chest of the bounty hunter. Moose Donovan was stopped in his tracks. He threw up his arms and toppled forward, to crash face downwards in the dust. There were two bloody holes in his back where the bullets had exited from his body. He lay quite still. One of Stone's shots had struck him in the heart and killed him instantly.

The Kentuckian now turned his attention to the first of his would-be assassins whom he figured had to be Moose Donovan's partner, the foxy-faced Eddie Winn. Again he peered cautiously round the corner of the water-trough. The sidewalk opposite was deserted. Stone scanned it carefully. There was but one place where Winn could be hiding. The door to the town's funeral parlour stood slightly ajar. Winn had to be lurking in the shadows beyond the door.

Stone grinned. The mortician could not wish for a more convenient corpse. He aimed the revolver at the open doorway, reckoning to hit his unseen target about chest-high. Swiftly, he loosed off three shots, swinging the revolver from left to right across the width of the doorway. Which of the three shots paid off, Stone would never know, but one of them surely did. Eddie Winn yelled and then staggered out on to the sidewalk, clutching his left shoulder. As the bounty hunter stepped out of the shadows, Stone rose from behind the trough and pumped his sixth and final bullet into him. The slug struck Winn in the nose, shattering it, deflecting upwards and lodging in his brain. He promptly collapsed backwards into the doorway.

Stone swiftly reloaded the Frontier Model Colt, then walked across and aimed the gun at the fallen gumnman. However, he did not need to squeeze the trigger a seventh time, for Eddie Winn was already a suitable case for the mortician.

The shooting, in a town as quiet and well regulated as Great Falls, naturally enough brought the citizenry running. And, amongst the first to reach the scene, was Marshal Jim Bell. The lawman glanced comtemptuously at both corpses before turning to the Kentuckian.

'Wa'al, Mr Stone,' he growled, 'guess these

coupla no-account critters jest had to try an' gun you down. I s'pose they ambushed you, huh?'

'That's right,' said Stone.

'The goddam lunkheads!' The marshal glared at Senator John Caine, who, together with the mayor and the banker, Fletcher Mulgrove, had just arrived upon the scene. 'I hope, Senator, that we don't have no more trouble when the rest of yore bounty hunters hit town,' he rasped.

Caine's handsome and usually imperturbable features wore a grim scowl. He did not look at all pleased.

'I told 'em to obey yore ordinance agin' carryin' guns, Marshal, an' I gave 'em orders to steer clear of you, Mr Stone,' he said, adding tersely, 'Don't worry, Marshal, I'll keep the others, when they do arrive, on a real tight rein.'

'You'd better.' John Caine might be a United States senator and one of Montana's richest and most powerful men, but Jim Bell did not give a damn. His first duty was to the citizens of Great Falls, and he proposed to execute this duty to the best of his ability. 'Any of those gunslingin' sonsofbitches give me trouble an' I'll run 'em outa town faster'n you can skin a rabbit. You got me, Senator?' he snapped.

'I got you, Marshal,' replied Caine. Then he turned to the Kentuckian and remarked, 'This gunfight has sure cost me. I'd hand-picked Moose Donovan and Eddie Winn. They was a pretty darned successful team.'

'Wa'al, unless you recruit a coupla replacements, guess yore complement's gonna be down to eight,' said Stone.

'I ain't got time to recruit nobody else,' said Caine. 'Still,' he added philosophically, 'I figure eight seasoned bounty hunters oughta be 'nough to tackle one stinkin' half-breed, even if he is plumb loco.'

'Mebbe,' said Stone.

The Kentuckian turned his back on the senator and, stepping across to where his gelding stood on the far side of the street, placed one foot in the stirrup. As he did so, the senator grabbed him by the arm.

'Wait a minute, Mr Stone,' said Caine. 'You surely ain't aimin' to leave town so soon? I thought you'd be stayin' overnight at least.'

'A change of plans, Senator.'

'So, you won't be actin' as scout on my expedition into the Little Belt Mountains?'

'Nope.'

'You'd be doin' the folks around here a mighty big favour. Injun Joe Brady is ...'

'Yore problem, not mine.'

'Now, that ain't exactly showin' what I'd call the right spirit,' protested Caine.

'Mebbe I don't feel like showin' the right spirit,' retorted the Kentuckian and, freeing himself from the senator's grasp, he swung up into the saddle.

'G'bye, Senator. G'bye, Marshal,' he said.

Then, before either man could respond, he dug his heels into the gelding's flanks and was off at a brisk canter.

FIVE

The six bounty hunters had travelled by train to Sheridan, Wyoming. They had started out from various different points, and it was only when they arrived in Sheridan that they realized they were all responding to Senator Caine's summons and heading for the Montana cattle town of Great Falls. They had met by chance in the bar-room of Sheridan's Elk's Head Hotel, whence they had repaired in order to take some refreshments after their long, wearisome train journey. Fast Freddie Randall from Denver had recognized Mickey Oakes and Ned Scranton from Springfield, Missouri, and had introduced himself. They had soon discovered they were engaged upon the same business, and the others, overhearing their conversation, had been likewise enlightened. The six had consequently teamed up and set out together on the long ride across the state line into Montana and on up through the wild frontier country to Great Falls.

It was now six days since the bounty hunters had left Sheridan. They were camped in the foothills of the Crazy Mountains and hoped to reach their destination in about another three days. They sat round the camp-fire, drinking coffee, smoking either cigarettes or cheroots and exchanging stories of past adventures. All of them knew that the price on Injun Joe Brady's head was $5,000, and Senator Caine's guarantee to double it and, into the bargain, pay all their expenses, more than compensated for the fact that the bounty would have to be divided six ways. They were men greedy for money, yet not one of them would have been prepared to ride alone into the Little Belt Mountains in pursuit of the half-breed. The legend of Injun Joe Brady had spread far beyond the borders of Montana, and his fearsome reputation was such as to put the fear of God into any man.

Fast Freddie Randall and the bounty hunter from Dodge City, Kansas, Gus Brown, usually practised their dangerous trade on their own, and had only responded to the senator's telegraph message because he had indicated they would not, on this occasion, be working alone. Antonio Garcia and Juan Valdes from Albuquerque worked as a pair, as did Mickey Oakes and Ned Scranton and, therefore, the senator had not troubled to inform them of this fact. All were mighty relieved, however, to be riding as a posse of six against the half-breed. Odds of six to one suited them just fine.

Of the six bounty hunters, only the two lone riders, Fast Freddie Randall and Gus Brown routinely considered confronting their quarry. The pairings of Garcia and Valdes and Oakes and Scranton much preferred to ambush their victims. Although all were engaged in the same profession, they were in fact a disparate bunch.

The youngest by several years was Fast Freddie Randall. He was in his early twenties, a tall, bold-looking fellow with a thatch of corn-coloured hair and a moustache to match. He was neatly attired in a black city-style suit and Derby hat, grey vest and white cambric shirt with a ruffed collar. And he sported not one gun, but two: a pair of pearl-handled Colt Peacemakers.

Gus Brown was a few years older, perhaps twenty-nine or thirty. He had served as a lawman before turning to bounty-hunting, and had only recently taken up his present profession. However, bringing in the two notorious hold-up artists, Madison Jones and Billy Bridgewater, both shot dead, had secured his reputation. Short and stocky, with an evil-looking, badly pockmarked face, he wore a grey Stetson and levis, and a check shirt and black leather vest beneath his long ankle-length brown leather coat. He sported a single Remington revolver on his right thigh.

Antonio Garcia and Juan Valdes could have

passed for none other than Mexicans even had they not been wearing wide-brimmed sombreros and colourful ponchos. They were much of an age, Garcia the taller and rather more handsome of the two. Neither looked particularly vicious, until one observed the look in each man's eye. The two Mexicans had killers' eyes, cold and pitiless. Compassion was not in their make-up. And, compared to the others in the party, they were remarkably heavily armed. Antonio Garcia carried a British Tranter in his right-hand holster, tied down on his thigh, and a .30 calibre long-barrelled Colt in a shoulder-rig beneath his poncho. He also had on his person no fewer than three razor-sharp knives, one in a sheath at his waist and the other two tucked into his calf-length brown leather boots. Juan Valdes was similarly armed, with the single exception of the .30 calibre Colt. Instead, he had a two-barrelled derringer hidden up the right-hand sleeve of his embroidered Mexican jacket.

The pair from Springfield, Missouri, Mickey Oakes and Ned Scranton, were easily the oldest of the six bounty hunters, both men being in their mid-forties. Of average height, yet powerfully built, broad-shouldered and square-jawed, and with their faces sprouting whiskers and heavy beards, they could easily have been taken for twins, except that, while Oakes's hair, whiskers and beard were gingery brown peppered with grey, Scranton's were as pure white as the snow still sprinkling the tops of the nearby Crazy Mountains. Each man wore dark city-style clothes and carried a Bowie knife and a Colt Peacemaker.

In addition to their handguns and knives, all six bounty hunters had rifles in their saddleboots, the four Americans favouring Winchesters and the two Mexicans Colt Hartford revolving rifles.

These, then, were the men whom Senator John Caine had selected to help him hunt down and bring to justice the half-breed whose killings had, for a period of just over three years, brought terror and foreboding to ranchers, cowboys, homesteaders and, indeed, almost everyone across the length and breadth of the State of Montana.

Antonio Garcia had just completed the tale of how he and Juan Valdes had succeeded in shooting dead the notorious Mexican outlaw, Pedro "El Lobo" Lopez, and the others were contemplating turning in for the night, when Fast Freddie Randall brought up the subject of their current assignment.

'I don't reckon,' he drawled, 'that Injun Joe Brady will prove to be anywhere near as easy meat as was El Lobo.'

'What do you mean?' demanded Garcia angrily. 'What are you implying?'

'I'm sayin' that El Lobo was a no-account sonofabitch who got by murderin' unarmed dirt-farmers, stealin' their paltry life-savin's an'

rapin' their wives. In between killin's, he was
rarely sober an', if ever he drew his gun, was more
likely to shoot hisself in the foot than anythin'
else.'

This remark brought a huge guffaw of laughter
from Fast Freddie's three compatriots. The two
Mexicans, meanwhile, glared angrily at the young
gunslinger. They possessed the natural haughty
pride of their race. Had they realized from the
beginning that Senator Caine expected them to
ride in a posse with a bunch of gringos, they might
well have refused his commission. However,
having come as far as Sheridan before discovering
this fact, they had decided to bury their prejudices
and continue on to Great Falls. On their ride from
Sheridan to the foothills of the Crazy Mountains,
the two men had been subjected to several barbed
comments, mostly from the mouth of Fast
Freddie. So far they had stifled their anger. But
his latest remark brought matters to a head.

The killing of Pedro Lopez had made them
heroes down in New Mexico. It was true that most
of the bandit's victims had indeed been dirt-
farmers. But that did not make him any the less
dangerous. He had had several confrontations
with the law and survived all of them. The
lawmen had not been so fortunate, for Lopez had
shot dead one deputy sheriff and badly wounded
three others. To call El Lobo a drunken
sonofabitch, who was as likely to shoot himself as

70

anyone else, was to insult not only the bandit, but also his vanquishers.

'You think you could have faced down El Lobo?' sneered Garcia.

'Seein' as how you two greaseballs managed to take him, guess I could, too,' replied Fast Freddie.

This comment brought both Mexicans scrambling to their feet.

'You withdraw that remark!' cried Garcia.

'Yes, or we show you how good we are with the gun!' added an enraged Juan Valdes.

Fast Freddie Randall continued to loll beside the camp-fire. He smiled indolently up at the two Mexicans.

'You gonna do that together, I guess? Odds of two to one appeal to you, huh?'

'Now look, Freddie, this ain't no way to ...' began Gus Brown, who did not like the way matters were developing.

'Jest keep outa this, Gus,' said the youngster coolly.

The man from Dodge City shrugged his shoulders and moved to one side. He sensed the inevitable and did not want to be in the line of fire when the shooting started.

Slowly, almost languidly, Fast Freddie rose to his feet. He guessed correctly that the two Mexican bounty hunters had taken Pedro 'El Lobo' Lopez by surprise, had probably shot him in the back. And he also suspected that, despite their show of bravado, they had little stomach for a face-to-face gunfight.

He was right. But the two men were committed. They could not afford to back down.

Antonio Garcia was the first to go for his gun. The British Tranter cleared leather and swung up in one swift, flowing arc. Juan Valdes followed suit a split second later. His revolver, too, swung upwards, its barrel directed at the young, blond-haired gunslinger. However, the youngster was not called Fast Freddie for nothing. His pair of pearl-handled Colt Peacemakers were blazing fire before either of the Mexicans' guns had completed their respective arcs.

Altogether, Fast Freddie Randall pumped six shots into his two protagonists, the three from his right-hand gun ripping into Garcia's chest, all within a two-inch radius. His left-hand grouping was not quite so tight. It was, though, equally lethal. Two bullets ploughed into Valdes' chest, while the third struck him in the throat, demolishing his Adams' apple and exiting through the back of his neck.

The young gunslinger strolled across to where the two Mexicans lay. Antonio Garcia was dead and his compadre was dying fast, crimson spurts of blood shooting up out of the wound in his throat. Fast Freddie Randall stared down at Valdes and smiled thinly. The fountain of blood would soon cease to spurt forth, and its cessation would mean that the Mexican had breathed his last.

'Hell, Freddie, did yuh need to provoke 'em into a gunfight?' demanded Gus Brown irritably.

'Never could stand them greaseballs,' confessed Fast Freddie. 'An' sure didn't wanta have to work with 'em.'

'Senator Caine ain't gonna be none too pleased,' remarked Ned Scranton.

'Sure ain't,' averred his partner, Mickey Oates.

'Wa'al,' said Fast Freddie, 'that's jest too bad.' He shrugged his shoulders and enquired, 'Any of you boys got a problem with what I jest done?'

'Guess not,' said Scranton. 'But this means there's only four of us left to go huntin' Injun Joe Brady.'

'So?'

'So, the risks are gonna be increased. There's safety in numbers. I've always believed in that maxim,' said Scranton.

'Wa'al, I reckon the odds are fine as they are. We ain't after no John Wesley Hardin, only some goddam half-breed. Ain't odds of four to one good 'nough for yuh?'

'Sure are, Freddie,' said Gus Brown.

The youngster grinned broadly.

'There you are then,' he drawled. 'An', 'sides, with me eliminatin' Sênors Garcia an' Valdes from our posse, the bounty is only gonna have to be divided four ways.'

Mickey Oakes and Ned Scranton exchanged

glances. They had no particular liking for Mexicans, but had been quite happy to have the pair ride along. They regarded Fast Freddie Randall's having provoked the shoot-out ill-judged and unnecessary. Nevertheless, they had no wish to quarrel with the youngster, and certainly the prospect of earning one quarter instead of one sixth of the bounty appealed to their sense of greed.

'OK. Let's bury their bodies an' then hit the sack,' suggested Mickey Oakes.

'We ain't got no spades,' retorted Fast Freddie.

'Wa'al, I ain't sleepin' beside a coupla corpses! Hell, no!' exclaimed Oakes.

'Me neither,' said Ned Scranton.

'Then you'd best take 'em a ways up that there gulch an' cover 'em with rocks,' said Fast Freddie.

And so it was settled. While Fast Freddie Randall and Gus Brown bedded down for the night, their two companions dragged the Mexicans' bodies a hundred yards or so up a nearby gulch and there buried them beneath a pile of stones.

At the same time that Fast Freddie was reducing the number of Senator John Caine's recruits heading north from Sheridan, another couple were heading south from Lethbridge. They made up the senator's original ten.

Rick and Dan Pearce had left Lethbridge two

days back, crossed the Milk River and the Canadian border that morning and were now fast approaching the small frontier town of Shelby. The proposed to spend the night there.

Although they were brothers, Rick and Dan Pearce did not look in the least alike. Rick Pearce was four years older than his brother and took after his father. He was a tall, gaunt-looking man, with a harsh, hawkish visage, fierce black eyes and a hot temper. Dan Pearce, on the other hand, had his mother's short, rotund figure and plump, smiling face. He was altogether more amiable and tended, in times of crisis, to calm down his irascible, abrasive elder brother. But he had no more scruples than the other. He, too, was quite happy to hunt down and kill a man for the price on his head.

The two brothers could easily have been taken for trappers or buffalo hunters, for they were dressed from head to toe in skins. Coon-skin hats, buckskins, moccasins and heavy bearskin coats had protected them throughout the long Canadian winter. Now they had discarded the bearskin coats, which were lashed across the saddles together with their bedrolls. Each man carried a Colt Peacemaker and a Bowie knife and, in his saddleboot, a Sharps rifle with telescopic sights.

It was dark by the time the pair rode into Shelby. They left their horses to be curried, watered, fed and rested at the livery stables, then made their way to the biggest of the town's three saloons, the Jack of Diamonds. They pushed their way in through the batwing doors and found themselves in a bar-room similar to hundreds across the length and breadth of the West. They observed the sawdusted floor, the scattering of tables and chairs, the bar-counter with its hammered copper bar-top, the couple of pot-bellied stoves, the spittoon, and the brass kerosene lamps hanging from the rafters.

There were few customers. Half a dozen locals were playing poker at a corner table. A couple of drinkers were chatting and smoking at another table, and there were three at the bar, including the town drunk, a short, red-faced, rheumy-eyed fellow called Sam Dalton.

'A coupla beers,' growled Rick Pearce.

'Comin' up,' said the saloonkeeper.

The two brothers threw back the beers at one draught and immediately ordered a couple more. As they waited for the saloonkeeper to pull them, the town drunk sidled along the bar towards them. He smiled ingratiatingly.

'You boys come far?' he enquired.

'Far enough,' replied Rick Pearce shortly.

'Don't I know you?'

'I don't reckon so.'

'I … I'm sure I've seen you two fellers somewhere.'

'Oh, yeah?'

76

'Yeah.' Sam Dalton eyed the brothers curiously. He searched his memory and, then, all at once, the answer came to him. 'Yo're the Pearce brothers, ain't yuh?' he demanded.

'Mebbe.'

'I know I'm right.'

'So?'

'So, what're yuh doin' here in Shelby?'

'That ain't none of yore goddam business,' snarled Rick Pearce.

'No, it ain't,' agreed his brother.

Sam Dalton grinned nervously.

'No offence, fellers, but I can guess. An', for the price of a bottle of red-eye, I can provide yuh with the information yo're lookin' for.'

Rick Pearce fixed the drunk with a speculative eye. He could tell the man that he and his brother were simply passing through on their way south. But he doubted if the man would believe him, since he had evidently some reason for thinking they were in Shelby for a purpose.

'OK,' he said, intrigued, 'you tell us why we're in town?'

Dalton smiled his crooked, drunken smile and wagged a grimy finger at the two brothers.

'Yo're bounty hunters, right?'

'Why should you think that?' asked Dan Pearce.

'I was in Carson City when you brought in the body of the outlaw, Frank Page.'

'We could've packed in that kinda work a long

77

while back,' said Rick Pearce.

'But you ain't?'

'Nope.'

'So, I reckon yo're here, aimin' to take in Bobcat McGraw.'

'Bobcat McGraw! Is he in town?'

'Aw, c'mon, that's why yo're here, right?'

'Wrong.'

Sam Dalton's jaw dropped.

'But ... but you've heard of Bobcat McGraw?' he muttered.

'Sure have. A mean bastard, wanted for murder in three states. Is he lyin' low here in Shelby?' asked Rick Pearce.

'Could be.'

'Could be?'

An avaricious glint entered the drunk's rheumy eye.

'You wanta know whereabouts in Shelby to find Bobcat, I'll tell yuh. For the price of a bottle of red-eye,' he croaked.

Rick Pearce laughed harshly.

'You drunken skunk!' he rasped. 'You'll tell us for nuthin'.'

So saying, the bounty hunter pulled his revolver from its holster and jabbed it into Sam Dalton's ribs.

'Hey, gents, I don't reckon you oughta ...' began the saloonkeeper.

'Shuddup an' keep oughta this!' growled Dan

Pearce, his hand hovering menacingly above the butt of his Colt Peacemaker.

'Yessir,' said the saloonkeeper, promptly deciding to leave Sam Dalton to find his own salvation.

'Wa'al,' said Rick Pearce to the drunk, 'where do we find Bobcat McGraw?'

All thought of a free bottle of red-eye had vanished. All Sam Dalton was concerned with now, was to save his worthless skin.

'He ... he's shacked up with the Widow Begg,' he stammered.

'An' whereabouts does the Widow Begg live?'

'The second-last white frame house on West Street. On the right-hand side.'

Rick Pearce dropped his gun back into its holster and turned to face his brother. They exchanged glances.

'Wa'al, Dan, whaddya think?'

'Fate seems to decree we go after Bobcat. After all, a bird in the hand....'

'That's true. An' this Injun Joe Brady could be hard to track down.'

'So, let's go git Bobcat.'

Rick Pearce placed a delaying hand upon the other's arm.

'Wait a second. What's the price on his head? D'you remember?' he demanded of the drunk.

'It ... it's five hundred dollars, dead or alive,' stammered Sam Dalton.

The two brothers again exchanged glances. This

was a lot less than Senator Caine had promised in his telegraph message. However, to earn the larger bounty, they first had to find and catch Injun Joe Brady. Bobcat McGraw, on the other hand, was not only unsuspecting, but also close at hand. A difficult decision.

In the event, the decision was made for them, for, while they were still mulling it over, Bobcat McGraw himself strolled into the saloon. He straightway recognized the two bounty hunters, turned and fled.

By the time they had run outside, the outlaw was already in the saddle and riding hell-for-leather out of town. The brothers cursed loud and long, before eventually returning to the bar, where they ordered another couple of beers. Pursuit was out of the question. They had no idea whence Bobcat McGraw was headed and could not possibly hope to pick up his trail in the dark. In consequence, Senator John Caine's posse was not, after all, reduced still further.

SIX

Jack Stone rode into the town of Medicine Hat as
dusk was falling. He had crossed the border into
Canada two days earlier and altogether it had
taken him five days' hard riding since leaving
Great Falls. He dismounted in front of the town's
only saloon, the Last Frontier, climbed up on to
the stoop and strolled in through the batwing
doors.

The Kentuckian pushed his way through the
crowd round the bar and ordered a beer. Then, as
he paid for his drink, he asked the bartender,
'D'you know if a feller, name of Jean-Pierre
Lapointe happens to live some place here in
town?'

'Who wants to know?' replied the bartender, a
short, swarthy individual in a grubby white
apron.

Stone fixed the man with his cool blue eyes.

'I do,' he snapped.

'And who might you be?' enquired the bartender

suspiciously.

'The name's Stone, Jack Stone.'

This evidently meant nothing to the bartender, who continued to regard the Kentuckian with a distrustful eye. Stone might be a legendary figure in Montana and across the West, but his fame had not yet spread northwards into Canada.

'*Alors*, Monsieur Stone,' said the bartender, 'will you tell me why you are enquiring about Jean-Pierre?'

'Ah, so he is livin' here in town!'

'Jacques did not say that,' remarked one of the drinkers at the bar, a large, heavily bearded mountain man.

'You spoke of him as though you knew him,' said Stone to the bartender.

'That does not mean he is here in town,' retorted Jacques.

'Then, where is he to be found?'

'I am not sure I can tell you that.'

'I don't mean him no harm.'

'No?'

'No,' Stone stared hard at the man. 'What the hell's goin' on here?' he demanded.

'I do not know what you mean,' replied the bartender.

'Aw, I think you do!' said Stone. 'Jean-Pierre Lapointe warned you all 'bout strangers ridin' into town an' askin' for him, didn't he?'

'*Peut-être*,' said a tall, buckskin-clad man,

pushing through the crowd and confronting the Kentuckian.

Stone unfastened his gun-belt and slapped the Frontier Model Colt down on to the bar-counter.

'You gonna take me to him?' he asked.

The other man looked Jack Stone up and down appraisingly. He was tall and lean, with a thick thatch of black hair and a neat black beard and moustache. Stone reckoned he was no more than twenty-seven or eight, although the beard made him look older.

'Wa'al?' said Stone.

The man's coal-black eyes continued to stare unblinkingly at the Kentuckian.

'*Certainement.*' He turned to the bartender. 'Is it permitted that I take Monsieur Stone into your parlour, Jacques?' he asked.

Jacques shrugged his shoulders.

'*Mais oui,*' he replied.

The tall man pulled out an ancient, long-barrelled .30 calibre Colt and pointed it at the Kentuckian.

'Through there,' he said, indicating a door which stood to one side of the bar and led into the saloon's rear quarters.

Stone made no attempt to retrieve the Frontier Model Colt, but simply turned and headed for the door. He pushed it open and found himself in a dark, narrow passage.

'Take the first door on your left,' said the tall man.

Stone did as he was bid and entered a small, sparsely-furnished parlour.

There was a fire lit in the grate, albeit a poor, cheerless, smoking affair, while on either side of the fireplace stood a couple of rather moth-eaten armchairs.

'Sit down,' commanded the tall man.

Stone chose the left-hand armchair. The tall man cautiously lowered himself on to the other and, his gun still trained upon Stone, sat facing him.

'What do you want with Lapointe?' he demanded.

Stone grinned.

'Let's stop playin' games,' he growled. 'Yo're Jean-Pierre Lapointe, ain't that so?'

The tall man did not return Stone's grin, but continued to stare stonily at the Kentuckian.

'Yes,' he said finally. 'I am Jean-Pierre Lapointe. How did you find me?'

'The marshal back in Great Falls told me you had a sister up here in Medicine Hat. So, I reckoned that, when you quit Montana, this was most likely where you would've headed.'

'Hmm. It seems then that I should have gone some place where nobody knew me.'

'Why?'

'You know why, Monsieur Stone.'

'Do I?'

'Of course you do.' Lapointe regarded the

84

Kentuckian with a cold, unwavering eye. 'You know,' he remarked, 'I never figured you for a bounty hunter.'

'You've heard of me, then?'

'*Naturellement*, Monsieur Stone. South of the Milk River, you are quite famous. But I heard you had given up gunfighting, had handed in your badge.'

'That's right. I aim to keep outa trouble these days.'

'I would not call bounty-hunting keeping out of trouble.'

'Yo're jumpin' to conclusions, Mr Lapointe.'

'Am I?'

'Yeah, for I ain't no bounty hunter.'

'*Eh bien*, there is no price on my head, so I suppose, in the strict sense of the word, you are not a bounty hunter. But you are a hired gun. Hired by Senator John Caine to hunt me down and kill me.'

'If 'n' I was, d'you think I'd've ridden into town like I did an' asked for you straight out?'

'I ... I....'

'I ain't exactly a fool, Mr Lapointe.'

'No, but....'

'Only a fool would've acted the way I did, knowin' that you was probably expectin' Caine to send someone after you.' Stone smiled wryly and added, 'You've been expectin' someone to come lookin' for you for jest over three years, ain't that so?'

Lapointe nodded grimly.

'If Caine did not send you, why are you here?' he asked.

'Wa'al, it was like this: I chanced to ride into Great Falls, where I was approached by the senator to act as guide on a li'l expedition he was plannin'. Seems he intends ridin' up into the Little Belt Mountains in pursuit of a half-breed called Injun Joe Brady. Brady's gone loco, y'see, an' has been rampagin' all over Montana, murderin' an' scalpin' folks.'

'Indeed?'

'You ain't heard?'

'No. How many people has he killed so far?'

'Eight. The last was a feller named Chuck Leney, some big-shot rancher who …'

'Do you know who else he killed?'

'I b'lieve the marshal told me one of 'em was the mayor of Lewistown.'

'Walter Flannery!'

'Yeah, I think that was the name.'

'Anyone else?'

'Some rancher called Richards.'

'And who else?'

'I dunno any more names.'

Jean-Pierre Lapointe laughed harshly.

'Eight down and one to go!' he cried.

'Whaddya mean?'

'Before I answer that, you must tell me why you are here? You said you were asked by Senator Caine to guide his expedition into the Little Belt

Mountains. But that does not explain why you came looking for me.'

'No, I s'pose not.'

'*Alors?*'

'Accordin' to rumour, Injun Joe Brady was a decent, law-abidin' hunter an' trapper till he lost his wife an' child in childbirth. The horror of that event seems to have turned his brain an' changed him into a savage, maniacal killer.'

'Yes.'

'So, me an' Injun Joe have got somethin' in common. I, too, lost my wife an' child in childbirth, and I went kinda crazy for a while. But I didn't go around scalpin' an' murderin' folks.' Stone looked the French-Canadian straight in the eye. 'I don't b'lieve Injun Joe is killin' folks at random like Caine claims he is. 'Deed I b'lieve there's a kinda link 'tween the death of Injun Joe's wife an' a certain huntin' expedition that Caine organized followin' his election victory in the fall of '79.'

'I see.'

'Marshal Jim Bell told me that you acted as guide on that expedition.'

'That is true.'

'Wa'al, I figured I'd try to find you, an' ask what happened up there in the Little Belt Mountains that fall.'

'You were not tempted simply to accept Senator Caine's offer?'

'Nope.'

'What kind of men is he planning to take with him up into the mountains?'

'He sent for eight seasoned bounty hunters, professional killers each an' every one of 'em.' Stone smiled grimly. He did not mention the two he had disposed of. 'Seems the senator is real anxious to track down an' kill this Injun Joe Brady,' he remarked.

'It would appear so.'

'Eight down an' one to go. What exactly did you mean, Mr Lapointe?'

'There were nine of them engaged on that hunting expedition in the fall of '79. I guess Senator John Caine is the only one still living.'

'Tell me about it.'

'It was a kind of spur-of-the-moment thing. The election had brought people into Great Falls from all over Montana. Then, when Caine won, there were great celebrations. It was in the midst of these celebrations that the senator took it into his head to set off with a bunch of friends into the hills on a hunting trip. Without more ado, he engaged me as guide, and we mounted up and headed out for the Little Belt Mountains.'

'You recall the names of his fellow hunters?'

'I do. There was Jake Richards and Walter Flannery and Chuck Leney, the three you already mentioned. Then there was a banker named Smith, and Bill Lloyd, a friend of the senator's from way back. And an army major named Pike, and a couple of ranchers from somewhere over near Helena, Don Henry and Pete Lorimer.' Lapointe smiled bleakly. 'If Injun Joe has killed and scalped eight people, I reckon they must be the eight.'

''Deed? So, tell me, what happened up in the Little Belt Mountains?'

'*Eh bien*, for the first three days, it was just like any other hunting trip. We shot a couple of grizzlies, a cougar and some deer, and the major, he shot himself a moose. All in all, a pretty good bag.'

'Yeah.'

'Anyway, on the fourth day, we headed back down towards Great Falls and, late that afternoon, just as we were thinking about making camp, we came across a clearing in the forest with a stream running through it. The ideal spot, only someone had got there ahead of us. There was a tepee pitched beside the stream. As we approached, a young Indian woman stepped outside. I recognized her at once as Injun Joe's Crow wife.' Lapointe sighed heavily and went on to explain, 'Injun Joe and I had been hunting and trapping up in those mountains for several years. Our paths crossed on many occasions and, more than once, I had shared a meal with him and Bright Feather ... that was his wife's name.'

'So, she also recognized you?'

'Yes, Monsieur Stone, she recognized me.' Again

Lapointe sighed heavily. 'She was so beautiful!' he said.

'An' pregnant?'

'*Mais oui*. She was very big in the belly. About eight months, I should say. Not that that made any difference.'

'Whaddya mean?'

'It was Jake Richards who started it. He was a big, coarse-grained fellow who, on previous nights round the camp-fire, had regaled us with a fund of the rudest, crudest stories imaginable. Anyway, he straightway declared that he fancied a tumble with Bright Feather. When she realized what he had in mind, she screamed and made to run for it. But it was of no use. He soon caught her.'

'Did nobody try to stop him?'

'I did.' The French-Canadian pulled his hair aside, where it flopped over his forehead, to reveal a livid white scar. 'The major laid me low with a blow from the barrel of his Army Colt. I don't know for how long I lay there senseless, but, when I came to, Bright Feather was sprawled in the grass, moaning and groaning, with Chuck Leney bouncing up and down on top of her. I protested and tried to drag him off. For my pains I received another crack across the head and was once again knocked unconscious.'

'The sonsofbitches!' rasped Stone.

'I ... I should have protected her,' said Lapointe, the distress showing only too clearly in his face.

90

Stone regarded the young trapper with a sympathetic eye.

'You did yore best. But, with odds of nine to one agin' you, I don't reckon yuh had a chance.'

'I suppose not, yet I feel guilty. I feel that, somehow or other, I should have stopped them.'

'How many of 'em raped her?'

'All nine.'

'Includin' the senator?'

'Yes. They boasted about it afterwards. Not one of them showed the least remorse.'

'So, what happened next?'

'We rode on down the mountain.'

'You went with them?'

'Yes, for I dared do no other. But that night, when eventually we made camp, I determined to give them the slip. And I did. As soon as they were all asleep. I saddled my horse and rode back up the mountain to where we had left Bright Feather.' Lapointe shook his head sadly. 'When I reached the clearing, I found Injun Joe had returned. He was cradling Bright Feather in his arms. She was in a bad way.'

'Injun Joe must've been distraught with grief?'

'*Mais oui*.'

'You told him what had happened?'

'I did.'

'And …?'

'He said nothing, other than to ask me the names of those bastards who had defiled his wife.'

The young trapper wiped away a tear, as he recalled that tragic night, before continuing, 'Bright Feather died just before dawn. I helped Injun Joe fashion a travois to take her back to her people on the Crow reservation for burial. Then, I headed north for Canada.'

'You didn't consider reportin' what had happened to Marshal Jim Bell or some other law-officer?' asked Stone.

'No. What was the point? Caine and the others were all men of influence. And they were white. Do you really believe any action would have been taken against them, Monsieur Stone?'

'I guess not.'

'That is why Injun Joe has taken the law into his own hands,' declared Lapointe.

'An' why Senator John Caine is so goddam keen to have him hunted down an' killed. He knows Injun Joe has avenged hisself on eight of 'em, an' he's afraid he'll be the next, him bein' the last on Injun Joe's list.'

'Yes. And, should the senator succeed in killing Joe, he will send a hired gun to kill me. That is what I fear.'

'But why?'

'Because of what I know ... and might tell.'

'But, hell, the folks down in Montana don't give a damn. Like most Westerners, they fear the red man an' look on him as some kinda vermin. Senator Caine could rape a dozen Injun women for all they cared.'

'His liberal friends back East in Washington might not take the same view, however.'

'I s'pose not.'

'They could well be appalled that he, a senator and a supposedly civilized man, should have not only failed to prevent the rape of Injun Joe's pregnant wife, but have actually participated in it. He might easily find himself ostracized.'

'An' he wouldn't like that.'

'No.'

'You've been convinced from the beginnin' that Caine would send someone to track you down an' kill you; ain't that right?'

'*Mais oui*. That is why Jacques was reluctant to answer your questions. I passed the word round Medicine Hat that I had made a powerful enemy back in Montana, someone who might hire a gunman to kill me. The townsfolk were to warn me should any stranger ride into town and ask where to find me.'

'You didn't tell 'em the full story, though?'

'No.'

'But why in tarnation did you come here? It was known in Great Falls that you had a sister in Medicine Hat. This was sure to be the first place Caine'd expect to find you.'

'I know.' The young French-Canadian smiled ruefully. 'I did not intend to stay. I came, meaning only to spend a few days with my sister, Marie, before moving on.'

'So what made you change your mind?'

'I met Violette. She was my sister's friend. She had arrived here in Medicine Hat to teach school while I was still down in Montana. We fell in love, married and now have a young daughter. Violette continues to teach school, and I make a decent living hunting and trapping. I cannot, and will not, cut and run.'

'I see.'

'*Peut-être* Injun Joe will outsmart these bounty hunters?'

'Mebbe. He has certainly done so in the past. But the senator said if 'n' I wouldn't act as guide, he had a Crow Injun in mind who would. An' there's no better tracker in the West than a Crow.'

'No, I guess not. So, now that you know the full story, what do you propose to do, Monsieur Stone?'

The Kentuckian eyed the trapper thoughtfully, then smiled and said, 'Cut out the "Monsieur Stone", will yuh, and jest call me Jack?'

'*Certainement*, Jack. And you will call me Jean-Pierre?' enquired Lapointe.

'OK, Jean-Pierre.'

'*Alors*, Jack, tell me, what will you do?'

'I guess I'll ride back down into Montana an' try an' find Injun Joe 'fore Caine an' his bounty hunters do.'

'And warn him?'

'Yup. An' if 'n' he wants to take 'em on, offer to

make a stand with him.' Stone paused and then asked, 'How 'bout you, Jean-Pierre, will you ride with me?'

'You say Senator Caine is taking an expedition of eight bounty hunters into the Little Belt Mountains to hunt down and kill Injun Joe?'

'Yup.'

'The odds favour the senator.'

'Yore comin' along would reduce those odds.'

'I know, but I cannot ride with you.'

'Cannot?'

'Will not. I am no gunfighter and, besides, I owe it to my wife and daughter not to go off and get myself killed.'

'Wa'al, I don't aim to git myself killed neither, not if I can help it.'

'Maybe not, Jack, but there is always that risk.'

'Reckon so.'

'*Eh bien*, it is not one I wish to take. After all, this is not my fight.'

'I guess you figure it ain't mine either?'

'No.'

'But I'm makin' it mine.'

The Kentuckian felt he could do no other. He appreciated only too well the dreadful pain and anguish Injun Joe Brady must have suffered. He could still, all these years later, recall his own feelings when his wife had died in childbirth. How much worse it must have been, he mused, when that death had been the result, not of natural causes, but of an horrific multiple rape. Stone determined, therefore, to help Injun Joe defeat the bounty hunters and exact his ninth and final revenge.

'It is with regret,' said the young trapper, 'that I must refuse to join you.'

''Course.'

Jean-Pierre Lapointe smiled sadly and lowered his revolver. He returned it to its holster.

'You will return to Great Falls?'

'No. I'll ride directly to the Little Belt Mountains.'

'When?'

'As soon as I've freshened up some.'

'*Alors*, why not stay the night? Come home with me. Violette will fix you a meal and you can enjoy a good night's sleep, then....'

'I dunno. I gotta git to Injun Joe 'fore Caine an' his gunslingers do.'

'You will travel faster if both you and your horse are fresh.'

Stone considered this point for a moment or two.

'OK,' he said eventually. 'Mebbe yo're right. Guess my hoss needs restin' up, even if I don't.'

'I shall take care of it for you.'

'Thanks, Jean-Pierre.'

The two men rose and shook hands. Then, they returned to the bar-room, where Stone retrieved his Frontier Model Colt from the counter.

'It is OK,' announced Lapointe. 'This man is not my enemy. *Au contraire*, he is my friend.'

SEVEN

At the same time that Jack Stone was crossing the Milk River on his way south towards the Little Belt Mountains, so Senator John Caine was strolling along Great Falls' Main Street in the direction of Mooney's Saloon.

Caine had become a hero, not only in Great Falls, but throughout the entire State of Montana, for he was the one politician who had made any attempt to bring to justice Injun Joe Brady, the half-breed whose series of savage killings had spread terror from the Cabinet Mountains to the eastern limits of the Yellowstone River. Caine had been the man responsible for sending, first a posse of US marshals, then a troop of US cavalry, off into the Little Belt Mountains in pursuit of Injun Joe. And now, here he was, planning to lead an expedition of bounty hunters up into those mountains at no little personal risk and expense. It was small wonder that the good folks of Great Falls treated him with a mixture of deference and adulation.

In the circumstances, it might have been supposed that the senator would be a happy man. In truth, he was not. The last of the bounty hunters had arrived and he had learned that their number was now reduced to six. Although six seasoned gunfighters ought to be more than enough to tackle one half-breed trapper, still Caine felt rather apprehensive. He had planned to take ten men with him. Too many? He did not think so. He believed strongly in safety in numbers. Nevertheless, he tried telling himself that six should be sufficient.

Caine was thus engaged when he found his passage blocked by the slim, dapper figure of Marshal Jim Bell. He pushed these thoughts to the back of his mind and greeted the lawman.

'Howdy, Marshal,' he said. 'Fine afternoon.'

'Sure is, Senator,' replied Bell. 'An' nice 'n' quiet. I hope it's gonna stay that way.'

'Whaddya mean?'

'I mean, Senator, that I don't want no trouble from any of them goddam lunkheads you've invited into town.'

'The bounty hunters?'

'Them's the varmints I'm talkin' 'bout.'

'Wa'al, Marshal, you can rest easy on that score.'

'I can?'

'Yeah. I've instructed 'em to make sure an' keep the peace.'

'As I recall, you gave them same instructions to Moose Donovan an' Eddie Winn. That didn't stop 'em tryin' to bushwhack Jack Stone.'

'That was jest unfortunate. If Stone hadn't hit town the same time as ...'

'Yo're puttin' that spot of trouble down to a chance encounter, huh?'

'Yeah.'

'Wa'al, let's hope we don't git no more chance encounters.'

'That's mighty unlikely, Marshal, partickerly since I aim we should set off at first light tomorrow.'

'In pursuit of Injun Joe Brady?'

'That's right. That's why I summoned 'em here.'

'I must say, it's real generous of you, Senator, doublin' the bounty an' all.'

'I b'lieve in lookin' after my constituents' interests. The cost to my pocket don't enter into the equation.'

'A noble sentiment.'

Caine glanced suspiciously at the marshal. Had he detected a hint of irony in the other's voice?

'As a representative of the people, I try to do what I feel to be right,' he said pompously. 'An' now, Marshal, if you will excuse me, for I have a meetin' scheduled.'

'With them there bounty hunters?'

'Yes.'

'Wa'al, be sure you impress on 'em to behave

theirselves.'

'I shall, Marshal, I shall.'

'G'day, then, Senator.'

'Good day, Marshal.'

The two men parted and, a few moments later, John Caine pushed open the batwing doors and strode into Mooney's Saloon.

It was late afternoon and the bar-room was fairly full. Caine observed the six bounty hunters sitting at a table near the window. He did not, however, go over to join them, but, instead, crossed the bar-room and entered a small room, set to one side of the bar-counter, which Noel Mooney hired out for various meetings. Caine had engaged it for his briefing with the bounty hunters.

The room was bare except for a single table, around which were set seven chairs, three down each of the longer sides and one at its head. Two bottles of Mooney's best rye whiskey stood in the middle of the table, and there was a glass in front of each chair.

Caine seated himself at the head of the table and poured a generous measure of whiskey into the glass in front of him. As he did so, the door opened and Noel Mooney stepped inside the room.

'You want I should show 'em in, Senator?' enquired the saloonkeeper.

'Show in Fast Freddie Randall on his own. I want a few words with him 'fore I speak with the others,' replied Caine.

'Jest as you wish, Senator,' said Mooney.

Caine did not have long to wait. He had barely sipped his whiskey before the door opened again and Fast Freddie Randall sauntered in. Caine eyed the tall, smartly dressed youngster up and down, and then gestured that he should take a seat. Fast Freddie did as he was bid and, following the senator's example, poured himself a whiskey. He raised his glass.

'To our success!' he said.

'I'll drink to that,' said Caine. Then, when they had both thrown back their drinks and replenished their glasses, he said quietly, 'I've got a bone to pick with you, Mr Randall.'

'Oh, yeah, Senator?' said the youngster.

'Yeah. You've reduced my party by two.'

'So?'

'That increases the odds agin' us killin' Injun Joe Brady.'

'Not by much. Even if we discount yoreself, there's still six of us to jest one of him.' Fast Freddie laughed harshly. 'You make sure we find him an' we'll kill him for sure.'

'Always supposin' you don't fall out with any more of my party,' rasped Caine.

'That ain't likely,' said Fast Freddie.

'No?'

'Nope. It's jest that I don't like greaseballs.'

'By that I s'pose you mean you don't like

Mexicans?'

'That's right, Senator.'

'Any other folks you don't like, Mr Randall?'

'Niggers, I guess.'

'How 'bout Injuns?'

'I feel like General Sheridan does 'bout them. What was it he said? The only good Injun is a dead Injun.'

'Wa'al, we got ourselves an Injun guide. A Crow called Red Knife. If 'n' we're to git anywheres near Injun Joe, we're gonna need Red Knife to track him down. You got that, Mr Randall?'

'Sure, Senator, I got that.'

'So, you don't go pickin' no quarrel with Red Knife. He ain't gonna be no use to me dead. An' we'll sure as hell never succeed in trackin' down Injun Joe without his help.'

'Aw, I don't know!'

'Wa'al, I do! Injun Joe knows those mountains like the back of his hand. Without Red Knife to guide us, we may as well stay here in Great Falls.'

The young gunslinger shrugged his shoulders.

'OK, Senator, you made yore point,' he conceded. 'I give you my word I won't pick no quarrel with yore pet Injun. Leastways, not till after we've disposed of the half-breed.'

He smiled slyly at the senator and Caine grinned back. If Fast Freddie wanted to pick a fight with the Crow *after* Injun Joe Brady had been tracked down and killed, that was his business. Caine could not care less.

'My only concern is that we put an end to the
'breed's rampagin' across Montana, killin' an'
scalpin' an' generally terrorizin' the good folks of
this state. You help me do that an', afterwards,
you can do as you goddam please,' he drawled.

'Oh, you can rely on me to kill him for you,'
averred Fast Freddie Randall.

'Good! Then, perhaps you'll do me a favour an'
call in the rest of my li'l expedition?' said Caine.

'My pleasure, Senator.'

The youngster rose and, retracing his steps,
opened the meeting-room door and beckoned to
the others.

Once they had trooped into the room, sat
themselves at the table and filled up their glasses
with whiskey, Caine began to carefully scrutinize
each of them in turn. He liked what he saw. Fast
Freddie Randall he recognized as a psychopath, a
born killer; not the kind of young man he would
normally wish to associate with, yet exactly the
right man for the job he had in mind. The
hawk-faced Rick Pearce and his younger brother,
Dan, both impressed Caine as men who
undoubtedly knew their business, as did the
veteran pair from Missouri, Mickey Oates and
Ned Scranton. As for Gus Brown, his evil-looking,
pockmarked countenance was enough to scare a
grizzly, let alone a human. Caine smiled. His
earlier doubts slowly receded as he viewed his

chosen team of bounty hunters. Surely this formidable bunch of seasoned killers would prove more than capable of dealing with one solitary half-breed? Assuming, of course, that Red Knife succeeded in tracking down their quarry.

'Wa'al, gen'lmen,' he said expansively, 'you know why I've invited y'all here to Great Falls. It's ...'

'I didn't know you was invitin' all these fellers along,' growled Gus Brown. 'You never said in yore telegraph that you'd sent for eight gun-fighters.'

'I could only include the bare bones of my offer. I couldn't go into detail. Surely you must see that?'

'Ten thousand bucks, that's what I thought was on offer,' said Brown, with a scowl. 'To be divided 'tween me an' one other.'

'I didn't intend to mislead you,' protested Caine.

'No?' muttered Rick Pearce.

'No, of course not.'

'We thought you'd hired jest us two,' said Dan Pearce.

John Caine decided there and then to make no mention of the two bounty hunters shot dead by Jack Stone.

'Look, boys,' he said, 'if 'n' you don't want this job, I'll reimburse yore expenses an' give yuh a li'l somethin' for yore trouble. I'm only lookin' for men who wanta ride with me.'

'It's jest that we don't like bein' hoodwinked,'

106

said Ned Scranton, stroking his snow-white beard.

'That was not my intention. Like I said, I couldn't go into a wealth of detail in a telegraph message. Hell, no!' Caine forced a smile and added, 'Anyways, even with the bounty bein' split six ways, you each are set to earn a tidy sum. One sixth of ten thousand dollars ain't to be sneezed at. An' I'm aimin' to pay all yore expenses. Nobody is likely to earn much less'n a coupla thousand dollars.'

The six bounty hunters exchanged glances. Then, finally, after a whispered consultation with his partner, Mickey Oakes threw back his whiskey and spoke.

'Me an' Ned, we're in,' he rasped.

A hurried discussion between the Pearce brothers followed. It, too, was conducted in whispered tones, while Caine waited expectantly.

'OK, Senator,' said Rick Pearce. 'Me an' my brother reckon, seein' as we've come this far, that we might as well ride with you.'

'An' me,' growled Gus Brown, though he still looked none too pleased.

Fast Freddie Randall laughed. He had never had the least intention of dropping out.

'You can count me in, Senator,' he said, with a grin.

Caine nodded. He had not really been worried that anyone would drop out. The six had wanted to air their grievance, their irritation that he had not been entirely honest with them. But he had figured that their avarice would far outweigh their pride and that, when it came to the point, none of them would be prepared to forfeit the chance to earn what was on offer.

'OK, boys,' he said. 'That li'l misunderstandin' bein' settled, let me tell you that we set out for the Little Belt Mountains tomorrow at first light.'

'That's where this Injun Joe Brady is holed up, huh?' said Fast Freddie Randall.

'Yeah.'

'You gonna lead this expedition, Senator?' enquired Gus Brown.

'That's my intention.'

'Why?' asked Dan Pearce.

'Yeah; surely, by doin' so, you'll be placin' yoreself in considerable danger?' added Mickey Oakes.

'I hope not. 'Deed, I'm relyin' on you fellers to protect me.'

'That still don't explain why yo're proposin' to lead the expedition,' remarked Dan Pearce.

'Because,' said Caine, 'I wanta be there when Injun Joe gits his. The murderin' sonofabitch has killed an' scalped some very good friends of mine, an' I'm lookin' for vengeance.'

'So, you ain't jest doin' this for political reasons,' commented Mickey Oakes.

'Nope.'

'There've been others, though, who have tried to hunt down this Injun Joe Brady; ain't that so?' said Gus Brown.

'That's right,' replied the senator.

'So, how come they failed?' enquired the man from Dodge City.

'Because none of 'em was familiar with the Little Belt Mountains, while to Injun Joe that territory is like his own backyard,' explained Caine, and he continued, 'That there posse of US marshals who went after him, they didn't even bother to engage the services of a guide. A real stupid mistake. Then, when a troop of US cavalry was despatched into the mountains, they took as their guide an old army scout called Marty Fitch, a feller whose trackin' skills weren't up to the job, partickerly since he's more often drunk than sober these days. And the third bunch to go lookin' for Injun Joe, a trio of bounty hunters, why they made the same mistake as did the US marshals.'

'I take it, Senator, that we ain't gonna make no such mistake?' said Rick Pearce.

'No, we ain't,' declared Caine. 'We've got ourselves the best possible guide, a Crow Injun called Red Knife.'

'An Injun? But ain't our quarry half Crow?' asked Ned Scranton.

'He is.'

'Then, are yuh sure this here Red Knife will be willin' to hunt down the 'breed?' enquired

Scranton.

'Oh, yeah, you don't need to worry on that score,' said Caine confidently. Then, eyeing each of the bounty hunters in turn, he remarked, 'Like I said, we ride out at first light. Until then, you boys are welcome to enjoy yoreselves at my expense. Only I don't want no trouble. Our town marshal ain't none too happy 'bout yore presence in Great Falls an', given the slightest excuse, will be only too delighted to run you outa town.'

'Mebbe we oughta test this here marshal? See if he's man enough for the job?' suggested Fast Freddie Randall, his eyes glinting mischievously.

'No,' said Caine. 'I forbid it. There's whiskey an' women a' plenty here in Mooney's. I repeat, enjoy both at my expense, but steer clear of the marshal.'

He glanced nervously round the table, and was relieved to see all except Fast Freddie nodding enthusiastically. The prospect of consuming as much whiskey as they could drink and having a tumble with one or more of Noel Mooney's sporting women, was a particularly pleasing one, and they were all quite happy to indulge themselves at the senator's expense.

'That suits us jest dandy,' said Gus Brown, boldly appointing himself as the others' spokesman. 'You can take it that there'll be no trouble. Ain't that right, Fast Freddie?' he demanded.

Realizing that his companions were all of the

same mind and anxious himself to enjoy the favours of the voluptuous Bonnie Regan whom he had already tumbled on his first night in town, the youngster shrugged his shoulders and grinned.

'Sure thing,' he drawled.

So it was that Senator John Caine left Mooney's Saloon a much happier man than when he had entered it. He had by now accustomed himself to the idea of hunting down Injun Joe Brady with a posse of six rather than ten bounty hunters. The men whom he had chosen seemed to be a pretty formidable bunch, and now all he needed to do was persuade the Indian, Red Knife, to act as their scout.

Since Red Knife was not at all keen to enter Great Falls, Caine had arranged to rendezvous with him at Lone Wolf Rock, a spot some two miles outside of town, where the trail forked.

Caine mounted his roan and cantered through the town and out on to the trail. The fact that Red Knife had agreed to meet him encouraged Caine to believe the Indian would accept his commission. He guessed, therefore, that, for some reason known only to himself, Injun Joe Brady had not informed Bright Feather's people of her rape and the part it had played in her tragic death. Had he done so, Red Knife would certainly not have contemplated helping Caine hunt down the half-breed.

It was almost dusk when the senator eventually

cantered up to Lone Wolf Rock, a huge granite formation that overhung the trail. As he approached, the tall, lean figure of Red Knife stepped out from the shadow of the rock. The Crow was clad all in buckskins, with a single eagle's feather protruding from his beaded headband. He carried a rifle and wore a large hunting-knife in a scabbard at his waist. Coal-black eyes gleamed above a huge, hooked nose. The Indian's face was gaunt, with high cheekbones and a wide, thin-lipped mouth, and his thick black hair hung down to his shoulders. A small racing pony was hobbled and munching the coarse grass beneath Lone Wolf Rock. All of this John Caine took in at a glance.

Caine swiftly dismounted and extended his hand.

'Glad you could make it,' he said.

'I said I would come,' replied Red Knife simply, as the two men shook hands.

'You have thought over my offer?' said Caine.

'Yes. Ten dollars a day to help your expedition hunt down the one you call Injun Joe Brady?'

'That's right.'

'What happens if we do not find him?'

'You still git paid.' Caine smiled and went on, 'But, if 'n' we do find him an' kill him, I'll pay you a bonus of one hundred dollars.'

Red Knife stared impassively at the white man.

'I shall want twenty dollars a day,' he said quietly.

'Ten dollars is pretty darned good!' protested Caine.

'But twenty is better,' countered Red Knife.

Caine reckoned he could scarcely dispute the logic of that statement.

'OK,' he said reluctantly. 'I'll pay yuh twenty dollars a day.'

'And for a bonus, I shall want two hundred dollars.'

Caine looked askance at the Indian. He had not anticipated Red Knife driving so hard a bargain. After all, he was not asking Red Knife to involve himself in the actual killing.

'I dunno,' he growled.

'You are asking me to help you track down someone of Crow blood.'

'Injun Joe's only half Crow.'

'Even so.'

'It's in the interests of the Crow nation that Injun Joe Brady be brought to book.'

'How is that?'

'Because some white folks are beginnin' to put the killin's down to Brady's Injun blood. They're pointin' out that not one of his victims has been a redskin, that they've all been respectable white folks.'

'So?'

'So, Red Knife, if 'n' we don't catch the 'breed soon, there could well be a backlash agin' yore people. I ain't sayin' it's right, but that's how it is.

113

Folks may take the law into their own hands an', for every white man Injun Joe Brady kills, string up a red man.'

There was a pause while Red Knife digested this information. Finally, after a lengthy silence, he spoke.

'I will accept one hundred and fifty dollars as a bonus,' he said.

'Done!' said Caine.

The two men again shook hands, this time to seal the deal.

'When do we set out?' asked Red Knife.

'Tomorrow at first light. My men an' I'll meet you here.'

The Crow nodded.

'Until we meet tomorrow, then, Senator.'

'Yes.'

Caine remounted his roan and headed back towards Great Falls. Behind him, the tall, lean figure of the Crow Indian remained standing motionless beneath the huge overhang of Lone Wolf Rock. Red Knife continued to stare after the senator until, eventually, Caine disappeared round a bend in the trail. Then Red Knife turned and slipped again into the shadows.

Senator John Caine, meanwhile, whistled a merry tune as he rode along. At long last, after a period of a little over three years, during which Injun Joe Brady had hunted down, scalped and killed each and every one of the senator's companions on the ill-fated hunting trip in the Fall of 1879, it seemed that his, Caine's, Nemesis was himself about to be hunted down and killed. With six experienced gunfighters to protect him and Red Knife to act as tracker, Caine felt confident that he would prevail against the half-breed. This time it would be Injun Joe Brady's scalp that was taken.

EIGHT

Almost the entire citizenry of Great Falls turned out to watch Senator John Caine and his party ride out of town. They, like the rest of Montana's population, believed Injun Joe Brady's killings to be the random acts of a deranged mind. Consequently, each felt that he or she could easily become the half-breed's next victim. None of them, therefore, ventured beyond the town limits unless necessity demanded. It was natural, in these circumstances, that the townsfolk should regard the senator as a local hero and his band of bounty hunters, whom they would normally have viewed with a mixture of fearfulness and aversion, as noble-hearted protectors. In consequence, as the small cavalcade proceeded on its way along Main Street, they roared their approval, cheering wildly and shouting words of encouragement.

The bounty hunters revelled in their new-found popularity. They smiled and raised their hats in salute. More used to being treated as a necessary evil, they were both surprised and delighted to receive such adulation. At their head, Caine smiled broadly. Ever the politician, he reckoned that there was scarcely one person in Great Falls whose vote he would not get at the next election.

Jack Higgins, together with Fletcher Mulgrove the banker and Dan Freestone the hotelier, stood on the stoop outside Freestone's hotel. As Caine and his men passed, the mayor raised his hat and cried, 'You bring in that murderin' sonofabitch an' I'll guarantee we'll have ourselves the biggest celebration Great Falls has ever known!'

'I'll keep you to that, Mr Mayor,' replied Caine, with a grin, as he rode on by.

Outside the law office, Marshal Jim Bell stood watching, flanked by his two deputies. But Bell did not raise his hat. Neither did he smile or cheer. He was glad to see the back of the bounty hunters, yet he was not at all sure that he wished them well in their enterprise. His chat with Jack Stone had set him thinking, and he was no longer convinced that Injun Joe Brady's killings were as random as everyone supposed.

Eventually, the cavalcade passed beyond the town limits and headed out along the trail in the direction of Lone Wolf Rock. There they found Red Knife waiting, mounted on his racing pony. Caine did not halt the party, but rode straight on. Without a word, Red Knife trotted out from the shadow of the rock and joined the senator at the head of the posse. Ahead of them loomed the jagged peaks of the Little Belt Mountains.

The camp-fire burned brightly, cheerfully even, though the men sitting round it and drinking coffee, had faces as gloomy as a winter's morning. They had been riding through that wild mountain territory for three weeks. This was to be their twenty-first night spent in the midst of the forests and ravines of the Little Belt Mountains, and so far there had been not the slightest sign of Injun Joe Brady. Their guide, Red Knife, had singularly failed to pick up the half-breed's tracks.

'We don't seem to be gittin' nowhere fast,' muttered a disgruntled Mickey Oakes.

'We sure don't,' agreed his partner, Ned Scranton, spitting despondently into the fire.

'Mebbe we should split up?' said Gus Brown.

'You fancy yoreself as a tracker, do yuh?' demanded Senator John Caine.

'He couldn't do no worse 'n' that goddam Injun! He's jest leadin' us round in circles!' declared Fast Freddie Randall.

Caine glanced over his shoulder to where the Crow sat, some way off from the others. If he had heard the youngster, he gave no indication.

'We cain't expect to hit on Injun Joe's trail straight away,' remarked Caine.

'Straight away! That's a joke! If 'n' we split four

ways, we'd have four chances,' said Brown.

'Four ways?'

'That's right, Senator. Me an' Fast Freddie, Mickey an' Ned, Rick an' Dan, an' you an' yore Injun pal.'

'I don't think so.'

'Why not? What Gus says makes sense,' interjected Rick Pearce.

Caine scowled. He was convinced that their only chance of success lay in Red Knife picking up the half-breed's trail. After all, none of the others was an experienced tracker. And, besides, Caine had no wish to lose the protection of the six gunslingers.

'We'll do it my way,' he said flatly, and, gambling that none of the bounty hunters would take him at his word, he added, 'Anyone who's unhappy 'bout this can lam outa these mountains whenever he darned well pleases.'

The six exchanged glances.

'We cain't be expected to roam these mountains forever,' commented Dan Pearce.

'We've only been up here a mere three weeks!' protested Caine.

'So, how long are you proposin' we carry on huntin' the 'breed?' enquired Ned Scranton.

'For as long as it takes.'

'That ain't good enough. I sure hadn't reckoned the sonofabitch'd be so goddam elusive, an' I don't propose spendin' months on end lookin' for him.

Hell, no!' exclaimed Scranton.

'Me neither,' added Rick Pearce.

Caine saw that he could soon have a mutiny on his hands.

'How long are yuh prepared to give it?' he asked anxiously.

'Another three weeks at most,' said Rick Pearce.

Dan Pearce nodded his agreement.

'The rest of you feel the same?' enquired Caine.

'Yup,' said Mickey Oakes.

'I reckon,' drawled Ned Scranton.

Gus Brown merely shrugged his shoulders. He did not like to give up on a job. Once he had embarked upon a bounty hunt, he liked to see it through. It was simply a matter of professional pride.

Fast Freddie felt the same. He smiled lazily and said, 'I guess I'll go along with the rest, Senator, though I cain't say I'm partickerly happy with our lack of progress.'

Caine nodded. He had to agree with the young gunslinger.

'Mebbe a change of tactics is needed,' he conceded.

'Whaddya have in mind?' growled Brown.

'Let me confer with Red Knife, an' then I'll tell you,' said Caine.

He rose and strolled across to where the Crow sat, calmly smoking his pipe and staring impassively out into the gathering dusk.

'I s'pose you heard what was jest said?' remarked the senator.

Red Knife nodded.

'Oakes was right. We ain't gettin' nowhere fast,' said Caine.

'No.'

'D'you reckon Injun Joe has spotted us?'

'Perhaps.'

'We ain't that big a party.'

'No.'

'But mebbe big enough?'

'It is possible.'

'So, if 'n' he has spotted us, whaddya figure he'll do? Jest keep a discreet watch on us till eventually we give up an' leave the territory?'

'That is what I should do.'

'So, like I said to the boys, mebbe we need to change our tactics?'

'Yes.'

'Hows 'bout if we stay put an' you head off on yore own an' try to pick up Injun Joe's tracks? Then, havin' located him, you could come back an' lead us under cover of darkness to where he's holed up.'

There was a short silence while Red Knife considered the senator's plan.

'Yes; I think that might work,' he said finally.

'Always supposin' Injun Joe don't spot you first.'

'He will not spot me. I shall take good care that he does not.'

'OK, let's give it a try.'

'Very well. I shall set off immediately.'

Caine looked and sounded surprised.

'This very minute?' he exclaimed.

'Your men are restless. It is best I do not delay.'

Caine smiled. 'I'll tell 'em,' he said. 'The news'll mebbe buck 'em up.'

He was right. The change of tactics and the prospect of a day or two spent lazing round the camp-fire cheered the bounty hunters considerably. Indeed, Caine himself was relieved not to have to saddle up the following morning. The constant riding through the mountains had proved pretty arduous, particularly for a man who was not normally used to spending hours on end in the saddle. Consequently, he was quite happy to indulge in a little rest and recuperation. His thoughts, however, remained with Red Knife. Caine prayed fervently that his new tactic would work.

Red Knife rode on up through the mountains. He was not sorry to leave Caine and the others behind. He had kept himself aloof from the bounty hunters and spoken only with the senator. However, as the days had passed and no sign had been found of their quarry, so the bounty hunters had become more and more morose and ill-tempered. Angry glances and muttered curses had been aimed in his direction, though nobody had actually picked a quarrel with him. He reckoned he had Caine to thank for that, for it was evident the others blamed him for their lack of success and would have dearly liked to tell him so. It was as well, therefore, that he had parted company with them. Indeed, he determined that, should he fail to track down Injun Joe Brady, he would abandon both them and Caine and head off back to the Crow reservation.

However, matters had not yet reached that pass. He still had hopes of earning the money promised him by the senator. On his own, he felt he was more than a match for the half-breed. He, too, knew the terrain, and he had the Crow's natural ability to travel silently and swiftly. If any man could steal up on Injun Joe Brady that man was Red Knife.

On several occasions, he had come across tracks, which might have been Injun Joe's, only to lose them. A mountain stream, or an expanse of rock, had intervened and he had failed to pick up the tracks again. Whether Injun Joe had realized he was being hunted and had deliberately sought to throw his pursuers off his trail, or whether his proceeding through water or across rock had been purely by chance, Red Knife had no way of knowing. It was quite possible that Injun Joe remained unaware that he was being pursued. After all, the Little Belt Mountains soared up out of a wild, untamed territory, consisting of deep forests, ravines, precipices, waterfalls, rapids and, in places, almost impenetrable undergrowth. In such country, Senator John Caine's small hunting-party might easily have escaped the half-breed's notice. Red Knife certainly hoped that this was the case.

The Crow pressed on all that day and the next, but still he failed to pick up Injun Joe Brady's trail.

It was on the third day that he struck lucky. At the foot of a narrow ravine, he came across the remains of a recent camp-fire. He studied it carefully and calculated that it had been extinguished no more than two hours earlier. Tracks, discernible only to the eye of an experienced tracker, led up into the ravine.

Red Knife had dismounted to examine the camp-fire. He did not re-mount, but, leading the racing pony by the bridle, proceeded on foot up the narrow defile. To his eagle eye, the tracks were clear and easy to follow. That they were those of some hunter or trapper he did not doubt. But whether that hunter or trapper was Injun Joe Brady, Red Knife had no idea. He followed the tracks with supreme caution, however, for he had no wish to become Injun Joe's latest victim, if the tracks were indeed his.

The long, arduous climb up the ravine took the best part of four hours, and it was almost dusk when Red Knife emerged to find himself at the top of a rocky incline, looking down upon a small forest glade. He hobbled his pony and crept through the tumble of boulders until he reached the edge of the incline. Peering down, he observed a tepee and a camp-fire and, drying on some nearby rocks, various animal skins. A pile of these were stacked in a rocky recess on the far side of the glade. Tethered and nibbling the grass were a small black racing pony and a mule. As he watched, a small, stocky man in buckskins stepped out of the tepee. Red Knife noted the long, jet-black hair, the hooked nose, the harsh, uncompromising features. At the same time, he noticed the lance stuck in the ground on the far side of the tepee. Tied to it were eight human scalps. His quest was over. The trapper was indeed none other than Injun Joe Brady.

It was clear to the Crow that, between killings, Injun Joe was continuing his profession as a trapper. Red Knife calculated that Injun Joe could not be intending to sell his furs at any trading post in Montana. His notoriety would ensure that he would be immediately recognized and thrown into jail should he attempt to do so. No, he must surely be aiming to head north into Canada with his furs. It did not add up. Injun Joe was supposed to have gone crazy, to have become a deranged killer, a madman, yet here he was apparently planning quite sanely to trade furs!

Red Knife pushed these thoughts aside. The point was he had tracked the half-breed to his lair. That was all that mattered. He now had a choice. He could either shoot the unsuspecting half-breed himself and claim the bounty, or he could lead Caine's cut-throat crew to Injun Joe's camp and let them do the deed and claim the bounty. Red Knife was tempted to pull out his rifle, take a bead on Injun Joe and squeeze the trigger. It was not the fact that Injun Joe had Crow blood that stopped him: it was the realization that Caine's bounty hunters would never let him live to claim his prize. They would kill him for sure. They had come a long way to earn that bounty, and would allow nobody, least of all a red man, to thwart them.

The Indian retreated backwards until he was far enough from the edge of the rocks to be out of sight should Injun Joe chance to glance upwards. He straightened up and turned, intending to unhobble his pony and return to Caine and the bounty hunters with the news that he had at last discovered Injun Joe's bolt-hole. But he found his passage blocked. The watcher had himself been watched. A tall, tough-looking stranger faced him. In the stranger's right hand was a revolver, and the muzzle pointed straight at Red Knife's heart.

'Seen enough, have yuh?' enquired the stranger.

'I ... I do not understand. Why do you point that gun at me?' cried Red Knife.

''Cause I'm tempted to shoot you.'

'But ... but why? I ... I am a simple hunter. I am

127

in these mountains hunting deer.'

'I don't think so.' The big man's eyes, cold and pitiless, fixed the Indian's in an unrelenting stare. 'Oh, yo're a hunter all right, but you ain't huntin' deer,' he said.

'Then, what am I hunting?' demanded the Crow.

'Yo're huntin' Injun Joe Brady,' replied the other calmly.

Red Knife gasped in surprise. He glanced towards his pony, at the rifle resting in its scabbard. Ten, fifteen yards away. He had no chance of reaching it before the white man fired. He fingered the hunting-knife at his waist.

'I wouldn't try pullin' that knife, not unless you want me to fill yuh full of lead,' said the big man.

'What … what do you mean to do?' asked Red Knife.

The big man smiled coldly. 'I figure we'll mosey on down into that there clearin' an' introduce you to Injun Joe.'

'But….'

'Git movin'!'

The Indian made no further effort to prevaricate. He recognized the note of finality in the other's voice, and had no doubt the man would shoot him dead if he did not obey. Followed closely by the gunman, he chose a narrow path that led down into the glade, where eventually he found himself face to face with the half-breed.

'Look who's come a-visitin',' said the big man.

Injun Joe Brady looked the Crow up and down for some moments.

'Wa'al, wa'al, I'll be doggoned if it ain't Red Knife. Now that *is* a surprise; ain't it, Jack?' he drawled.

'Not really,' replied Stone, for the Crow's captor was none other than the Kentuckian.

Injun Joe laughed: a harsh, mirthless laugh.

'I've been expectin' you,' he said.

'Expectin' me?' exclaimed Red Knife.

'Yeah. This here's a friend of mine, Jack Stone. He rode up into these mountains to warn me 'bout Senator John Caine's li'l hunting-party. Said that Caine had spoken of takin' a Crow brave named Red Knife as a guide.' Injun Joe fixed the Indian with an angry stare. 'You deny this?'

Red Knife shook his head.

'No,' he said, 'I do not deny it.'

'But why, Red Knife? I know we weren't exactly bosom pals, yet I do have Crow blood in my veins, an' Bright Feather, she was a full-blooded Crow. To help that sonofabitch, Caine, hunt me down for a few measly dollars....'

'It wasn't just the money.'

'No?'

'No. Caine said that the white men were beginning to blame the killings on your Crow blood. He reckoned there could be a backlash against my people, that for every white man you killed in future, they would string up a Crow Indian.'

129

'An' you believed him?'

'Yes.'

'Still, you didn't offer yore services free, did yuh? You demanded blood money.'

'Not for me. My people on the reservation are cheated by the government agents. The food we are promised often does not come, or, even when it does, the quantity is cut. So, I proposed to use the money received from Senator Caine to purchase food for my people.'

'That a fact?'

'Yes, it is.' Red Knife glared at the half-breed. 'You cannot expect me to put you before the good of my people. I know Bright Feather's death brought you great pain and unhappiness. Yet I cannot understand what possessed you to turn killer and ...'

'You don't know?' exclaimed Stone, glancing enquiringly at Injun Joe.

'No. What ... what is there to know?' asked Red Knife.

'You didn't tell Bright Feather's folks how she died?' Stone demanded of the half-breed.

Injun Joe sighed. 'No,' he said, 'I did not. I told them only that she had died givin' birth to our stillborn son. I did not want them to know that she had been defiled by those white bastards!'

'Defiled!' cried Red Knife.

'Yes. She was raped by a party of white hunters. Nine of 'em, includin' yore friend, the senator. It

130

didn't matter to them that she was pregnant an' close to her time.'

'Ah, I see!'

'Do you, Red Knife?'

'Yes. The eight men you have killed so far were all members of that hunting-party.'

'An' the sole survivor is Senator John Caine,' interjected Stone.

'But not for much longer,' added Injun Joe grimly.

'If I had known, I would not have taken his money. I would have refused to scout for him,' said Red Knife.

'Him an' how many others?' demanded Stone. 'Caine told me he was reckonin' on takin' along ten bounty hunters, only two of 'em tangled with me an' got theirselves shot. Did he recruit a coupla replacements?'

'No. In fact, he seems to have lost another two,' replied Red Knife.

'There are six of 'em?' said Injun Joe.

'Yes. Six and also, of course, Senator Caine.'

'Who are they?' growled Stone.

'There are two brothers, Rick and Dan Pearce; and the others are Gus Brown, Ned Scranton, Mickey Oakes and a youngster named Fast Freddie Randall.'

'D'yuh know any of 'em, Jack?' Injun Joe enquired of the Kentuckian.

Stone nodded.

131

'I don't know nuthin' 'bout the Pearce brothers,' he said. 'But I've heard of the rest. Fast Freddie an' Gus Brown usually work alone. A coupla loners, an' both as dangerous an' deadly as any copperhead. Ned Scranton an' Mickey Oakes allus work as a team. They specialize in shootin' folks in the back.'

'A nice bunch,' commented Injun Joe.

'But I reckon we can take 'em,' said Stone. He turned to Red Knife. 'Whereabouts are they?' he snapped.

'I left them camped at a point half-way up Wolf Mountain and below the tree-line. Just beneath Three Sisters Rocks, there is a small clearing with a stream running through it.'

'I know the spot,' said Injun Joe. His eyes glinted venomously. 'Let's go git 'em!' he snarled.

'But what are we gonna do 'bout Red Knife here?' demanded Stone.

'I'll go with you. I'll guide you to Caine's camp,' volunteered the Crow.

'We don't need no guide,' snapped Injun Joe.

'The odds against you, when you reach Three Sisters Rocks, will be seven to two. I could reduce those odds to seven to three.'

Injun Joe glanced at the Kentuckian.

'Whaddya think?' he asked.

Stone smiled thinly and shook his head.

'No.'

'Why not?'

'Red Knife was gonna take Caine's blood money to hunt you down.'

'But he explained his reasons.'

'Mebbe.' Stone stared curiously at the half-breed. 'You gonna forgive him, Joe?'

'I b'lieve so.'

'Wa'al, all I can say is, you've got one helluva forgivin' nature.'

'You know I ain't got that. Otherwise I'd never have taken to ridin' the vengeance trail. Then Caine an' them other....'

'Nobody could forgive them bastards!'

'No. No, yo're right there.' Injun Joe turned to face the Crow. 'If Jack don't want you along, guess that's good 'nough for me,' he said.

'I shall return to the reservation, then. And, now that I know that those eight killings were just, I wish you well in your attempt to finish what you have begun.'

'Thanks, Red Knife.'

'Yo're gonna jest let him go?' rasped Stone.

'I guess. I swore to kill Caine an' his pals, but I didn't reckon to kill nobody else. I cain't shoot Red Knife in cold blood,' remarked the half-breed.

'But he could go warn Caine that we're comin'!' exclaimed the Kentuckian.

'You have my word as a Crow brave that I shall not, that I shall ride directly from here to the reservation.' Red Knife smiled and added, 'I shall tell nobody what I have seen and heard today.'

'An' how will yuh explain yore return alone?' asked Stone.

Red Knife thought for a few moments.

'I shall say that, owing to our lack of success, Senator Caine dismissed me, and that he and his men are continuing their search without a guide.'

'I see. Wa'al, I s'pose that sounds feasible,' Stone admitted wryly.

'So, do we let him go, Jack?' asked Injun Joe.

'Me, I'd truss him up good'n tight, an' leave him here until after we've settled with Caine.'

'But, in the meantime, a grizzly, or a cougar, or a pack of wolves could come along!' protested the Indian, his eyes filled with alarm.

'That's a chance we'd have to take,' said Stone.

'I don't think so, Jack,' said Injun Joe. 'Red Knife has given me his word as a Crow brave. That's good 'nough for me.'

The Kentuckian shrugged his shoulders.

'If'n' you say so, Joe,' he said. Then, aiming his Frontier Model Colt at the Crow, he snarled, 'You doublecross us, Red Knife, an' yo're a dead man!'

Red Knife raised his arms in a gesture of reconciliation.

'I have given my word,' he said simply.

Thereupon, he turned and climbed slowly, and with dignity, back up the narrow path to where he had left his pony. He unhobbled the animal and mounted in one bound. Then, he swung the pony's head round, and digging his heels into the beast's flanks, disappeared from view.

Stone stepped across the clearing and entered the forest. Moments later, he returned, leading his bay gelding, which he had earlier hidden amongst the trees.

'OK, Joe, let's git goin',' he said.

'Yo're sure you wanta go through with this?' enquired Injun Joe. 'It ain't yore fight, after all.'

'Yo're gonna need me.'

'Ah, I guess so! As Red Knife jest pointed out, the odds are kinda agin' us. D'yuh reckon we can take all seven of 'em, Jack?'

'I reckon so.'

'But will you leave Senator John Caine to me?'

'You bet yore sweet life I will!' declared Stone.

NINE

Four days had passed since the departure of Red Knife, and the six bounty hunters were getting restless. Although they had agreed to remain in the mountains for a further three weeks, the lack of action caused by the absence of their scout had begun to affect all of them badly. Even Caine himself was feeling fidgety. He realized that Red Knife had a huge expanse of wild, untamed territory to cover, and that his search for Injun Joe Brady could take weeks, if not months. Nevertheless, he had hoped that the Indian working alone would have enjoyed an early success.

He glanced up at the mid-morning sky. There was not a cloud to be seen. At least the weather had been kind and, since the advent of May, the days had become warmer and the nights milder. He watched the others, who, for the want of something to do, were busily cleaning and examining their guns.

'Whose turn is it today to shoot us somethin' to eat?' he enquired.

'It's Mickey's, but neither he nor his pardner are worth a red cent when it comes to killin' somethin' for the pot,' remarked Fast Freddie Randall.

Mickey Oakes glowered at the youngster.

'Me an' Ned, we ain't no plainsmen. Never claimed to be,' he retorted.

'Neither am I,' said Fast Freddie. 'But that don't mean I cain't find me a deer, or a rabbit, or somethin' for the pot. Hell, this forest's teemin' with game!'

'You wanta go huntin' in my place, yo're welcome,' said Oakes.

'Why not, Freddie?' said Caine, hurriedly intervening to prevent any quarrel. 'Yo're 'bout the best hunter we've got,' he added silkily.

Fast Freddie Randall grinned and rose jauntily to his feet. Ever susceptible to flattery, he was happy, indeed eager, to prove worthy of the senator's commendation.

'OK,' he said. 'I'll see if I can find us a plump young deer for supper.'

'Hmm, I'd rather sink my teeth into a nice, juicy beefsteak,' remarked Gus Brown.

'Wa'al, there ain't no cattle up here in the mountains, Gus,' laughed Fast Freddie. 'So, I guess you'll have to make do with whatever I can catch.'

'Guess so, Freddie. But I'm sure as hell gonna

have me the biggest juiciest beefsteak you ever did see, the moment I git back to Great Falls!' declared the man from Dodge City.

'Me, too!' cried Mickey Oakes.

'Wa'al, that ain't the first thing I'm gonna have when we hit town,' said Ned Scranton.

'No?' said Oakes.

'No, pardner. I'm gonna have me one of Noel Mooney's whores. Any one of 'em'll do jest dandy.'

Rick Pearce roared with laughter and slapped his thigh.

'I'm with you, Ned!' he yelled.

'So am I!' exclaimed his brother.

'What about you, Freddie?' asked Gus Brown.

But he received no answer, for, while they had been talking, the youngster had slipped away. The bounty hunters' horses were hobbled on the northern edge of the clearing, immediately beneath Three Sisters Rocks. Fast Freddie had not troubled to saddle his sorrel, but had set off on foot, carrying the Winchester which he had just finished cleaning.

Senator Caine smiled broadly.

'Knowin' Fast Freddie, I reckon we're gonna eat well tonight,' he said.

In fact, Caine had little or no interest in supper. All he wanted was for Red Knife to return with news of Injun Joe's whereabouts. Then he could unleash the bounty hunters and rid himself forever of the vengeful half-breed.

Fast Freddie Randall, meanwhile, had vanished amongst the trees fringing the eastern edge of the clearing.

The youngster proceeded quietly, cautiously, into the forest. He was careful to note certain landmarks as he went, for he had no wish to become lost. However, at the same time, he kept his eyes and ears open for any sign of game. The sun's rays filtered down through the foliage making it pleasantly warm. Fast Freddie Randall smiled to himself. He enjoyed hunting, whether his prey was man or beast. The kill was what he liked best of all. That gave him a thrill like no other.

Randall's cautious, step-by-step progress through the trees brought him to another small clearing. It was about half an hour since he had left the others, and yet he was no more than half a mile from their camp. He peered across the clearing, hoping to glimpse a deer amongst the trees on its far side. Nothing stirred. Silently, Fast Freddie made his way across the open space. Above him the sun beat down relentlessly, its rays no longer deflected by the trees' foliage. Fast Freddie removed his black Derby and mopped his brow. Not for the first time, since embarking upon the hunt for Injun Joe Brady, did he wish he had exchanged his city-style garb for something more appropriate.

As the youngster replaced the hat on his head, a

slight movement caught the corner of his eye. He turned to see two men emerge from the trees on his left. One was small and stocky and clad all in buckskins, the other tall and broad-shouldered and wearing a buckskin jacket and levis. The smaller man, who was dark-skinned and hawk-faced, stared at Fast Freddie with fiercely glittering eyes.

'You lookin' for me?' he snapped.

'I ... I was huntin' game,' stammered the surprised youngster.

'You don't look like no hunter to me,' said the small man. 'Does he look like a hunter to you, Jack?' he enquired of his big, tough-looking companion.

'He sure don't,' said Jack Stone. 'Leastways, not a decent, honest-to-God hunter. 'Course he could be a stinkin', low-down bounty hunter, I s'pose.'

'Yeah,' drawled Injun Joe. 'Wa'al, are you a bounty hunter an' if 'n' you are, who are yuh huntin'?'

Fast Freddie glanced from one man to the other. He had never seen his quarry, but Injun Joe Brady had been described to him as a short, hook-nosed half-breed. The small man fitted that description exactly. But who, then, was his companion?

'Are you Injun Joe Brady?' he asked.

'I am,' said the small man.

'Then, I've been lookin' for you.'

'To kill me?'

'Yeah.' Fast Freddie turned his attention to the Kentuckian. 'I ain't got no quarrel with you, stranger,' he said. 'So, if you'll jest step aside....'

'I cain't do that,' replied Stone.

'Whaddya mean?'

'I mean, I'm with Injun Joe. You wanta kill him, you gotta kill the both of us.'

'Two to one, huh? They ain't exactly fair odds.'

'A darned sight fairer than the odds you was proposin' to give Injun Joe. Seven to one, if 'n' you count Senator Caine.'

'You ... you know 'bout the senator's expedition?'

'We sure do.'

'We've been spyin' on yore camp from a position up top of Three Sisters Rocks,' explained Injun Joe Brady.

'I must say I was expectin' Caine to have mustered a force of eight, mebbe ten, gunmen,' added Stone.

'There was to be eight of us, but me an' a coupla Mexicans had a slight quarrel.' Fast Freddie paused, and then added with a grin, 'By the time it was resolved, they was both dead an' the senator's party was reduced to six.'

He smiled menacingly. The thought of how easily he had despatched Antonio Garcia and Juan Valdes gave his ego a sudden boost. He studied the two men. Injun Joe, he knew, was a trapper and a hunter, but no gunfighter. Although the half-breed had accounted for eight men so far, not one of them had been particularly adept with a gun. The youngster reckoned, therefore, that he could, in all likelihood, easily out-shoot Injun Joe. As for the big man, he was probably just another mountain-man.

Since he was still clutching the Winchester in his left hand, Fast Freddie went for the pearl-handled Colt Peacemaker in his right-hand holster. Usually, he drew, aimed and fired his gun in one swift, fluid movement. On this occasion, though, he hesitated for one split second, unsure for a moment whom he should fire at first. That delay, momentary though it was, proved fatal. Before he could squeeze the trigger, the first of Stone's shots struck him in the chest.

The Kentuckian pumped three bullets into the youngster in quick succession. The first caved in three ribs and lodged against his spine, the second hit him in the belly, and the third blasted straight through his skull, exiting in a cloud of brains and blood. Fast Freddie Randall was dead even before he hit the ground.

'Holy cow. Yo're darned quick on the draw!' exclaimed Injun Joe. 'Me, I never even cleared leather.'

'Gunfightin' was my trade once,' replied Stone, as he proceeded to reload his Frontier Model Colt in preparation for the gun-fight yet to come.

The two men stared down at the prostrate form

of the young bounty hunter. In death he looked little more than a boy. It was difficult to credit that, in his short life, he had deliberately, callously, gunned down no fewer than a dozen men.

'OK, Jack,' said the half-breed, 'guess we'd best git our hosses an' head for Caine's camp.'

'Yeah. Let's go finish the job,' said Stone.

Gus Brown looked up in alarm when he heard the three shots. He laid down the Winchester, which he had been cleaning, and glanced at the others sitting round the camp-fire.

'Them's gunshots,' he rasped.

'So? I reckon Fast Freddie's spotted some kinda game an' taken a few pot-shots at it,' said Ned Scranton unconcernedly.

'Those weren't no rifle-shots.'

'You sure?' growled Scranton.

'I can tell the difference 'tween the bark of a rifle an' the roar of a hand-gun,' said Gus Brown.

'Hmm. Then, you got sharper hearin' than me,' confessed Rick Pearce.

'An' me,' added his brother, Dan.

'Anyways, what of it?' demanded Mickey Oakes. 'So, Fast Freddie fired his Peacemaker instead of his Winchester. Surely that ain't no big deal?'

'He took the Winchester with the intention of usin' it to shoot us our supper,' said Brown.

'An' evidently changed his mind,' said Senator

John Caine. 'Is that so very surprisin'?'

'Guess not,' muttered Brown.

But the man from Dodge City was not convinced. His instincts told him that something was wrong. Consequently, he removed himself from his position near the camp-fire and settled down instead amongst a tumble of boulders at the foot of the bluffs known as Three Sisters Rocks. Protected from attack from above by the overhang, Gus Brown had picked the only spot in the entire clearing that afforded any cover whatsoever.

Meanwhile, the others chose to remain in the vicinity of the camp-fire. Their instincts, unlike Brown's, had clearly not alerted them to any imminent danger. It came as a rude shock, therefore, when the first shot rang out.

Injun Joe Brady opened up with his Winchester from the top of Three Sisters Rocks. His first shot struck Ned Scranton in the chest and knocked him backwards into the camp-fire. As Scranton screamed and scrambled to escape from the burning embers, the others ran for cover. Not all of them reached it. Mickey Oakes and Dan Pearce were both cut down by Jack Stone shooting from the forest on the opposite side of the clearing to the bluffs, while Rick Pearce took the half-breed's second shot in the thigh. Only the senator succeeded in escaping into the tumble of boulders, where Gus Brown was hiding.

Mickey Oakes and the younger of the Pearce Brothers lay lifeless on the sward. Stone's two shots had killed them outright, one blasting Oakes's brains through the back of his head and the other penetrating Dan Pearce's black heart. Ned Scranton and the elder Pearce brother, meantime, each made a last, desperate attempt to reach cover.

Ned Scranton, with hair and clothes blazing, was screaming and trying to beat out the flames. At the same time, he set off on a weaving, tottering run towards the shelter of the boulders beneath Three Sisters Rocks. He was twenty yards away when Injun Joe Brady's third shot struck him between the eyes and once more knocked him flat on his back. This time he lay quite motionless, the flames still licking his lifeless body.

Rick Pearce was no more fortunate. The half-breed's bullet had broken his femur. Consequently, the slightest movement caused him to cry out in agony. Nevertheless, knowing that he was a dead man unless he reached cover, he attempted to drag himself across the clearing. He had managed no more than a few yards when another shot from Jack Stone laid him low. Neither he nor his brother would ever again claim another bounty.

A terrified Senator John Caine crouched down amongst the boulders. Fear had tied his stomach in knots and rivulets of cold sweat seeped down his back. His face ashen and his eyes wide with terror. Caine was barely recognizable as the affluent, powerful and seemingly imperturbable politician so recently fêted as a hero in Great Falls. He glanced nervously at the bounty hunter crouching beside him.

'What ... what in tarnation's goin' on?' he stammered.

'I reckon we've found Injun Joe. Or mebbe I should say, he's found us!' rasped Gus Brown.

'But those shots came from all directions!' protested the senator.

'From jest two directions,' Brown corrected him.

'Even so, Injun Joe cain't be in two places at once.'

'No.'

'So?'

'So, he's got hisself an ally.'

'But who in hell would side with that savage, murderin' breed?'

'Yore guess is as good as mine, Senator.'

Caine was much too confused and fearful to make any guesses. Anyway, more important than the identity of Injun Joe Brady's partner was the question of how he was going to escape the half-breed's revenge.

'Wa'al, what are we gonna do?' he demanded nervously.

'Sit tight,' said Brown.

'Sit tight?'

'That's what I said.'

'But we cain't stay here indefinitely.'

'You got a better idea, Senator?'

'No, but....'

'We sit tight till it gits dark. Then we make a break for it.'

'But dusk's hours away!'

'I know.'

Caine considered Gus Brown's plan. He had no wish to remain for several hours crouching at the foot of Three Sisters Rocks while Injun Joe Brady and his friend took pot-shots at them. An unlucky ricochet and he could easily end up dead. Nonetheless, he could think of no alternative plan.

'When we do make a break for it, whaddya have in mind?' he enquired. 'A quick dash for our hosses?'

He looked towards the horses which were hobbled only a few yards away beneath the bluffs. Then he gasped in dismay. Their saddles were scattered round the camp-fire in the centre of the clearing. Gus Brown followed his gaze and smiled bleakly.

'If we're gonna git away on them there hosses, reckon we'll needs ride 'em bare-back,' said the bounty hunter.

'But I ain't never rode a hoss bare-back before!' exclaimed Caine.

'Wa'al, I guess this is as good a time as any to start,' said Brown.

'You ... you'll stick with me, won't yuh?' cried Caine.

Gus Brown eyed the senator thoughtfully.

"Course I will,' he said, before adding with a crooked grin, 'for a price.'

'A price?'

'Yeah. Let's say five thousand bucks if 'n' I git you safely back to Great Falls.'

So great was Senator John Caine's fear of what Injun Joe might do if he caught him that he made no quibble.

'Done!' he said.

The two settled down to await the onset of darkness and, as they had anticipated, found themselves obliged to keep their heads low, for, throughout the rest of the morning and early afternoon, Injun Joe and Jack Stone pinned them there with sporadic bursts of gunfire.

Since the overhang prevented him from firing directly into the tumble of boulders, Injun Joe had clambered down from the top of the bluffs. He was now crouching amongst the trees on the opposite side of the clearing, and a few yards to his right was the Kentuckian. They took it in turn to pepper Caine's and the bounty hunter's refuge with rifle-fire. By early afternoon, though, it had become clear that these tactics were unlikely to force their quarry out of their bolt-hole.

'Those sonsofbitches ain't gonna budge, goddam 'em!' ejaculated the half-breed angrily.

'Don't reckon they are,' replied Stone.

'So, what do we do?'

'We can jest wait.'

'Starve 'em out, you mean?'

'I don't think it'll come to that. My guess is, they'll try an' make a break for it once it gits dark.'

Injun Joe peered anxiously across the clearing towards the tumble of boulders. Behind the boulders, Three Sisters Rocks rose sheer and perpendicular. There was no escape that way. His eyes ran along the foot of the cliffs to where Caine's and the bounty hunter's horses stood hobbled.

'Them hosses. If 'n' they git to them hosses....'

'They'll have to ride 'em bare-back.'

Injun Joe followed the Kentuckian's gaze. The various saddles lay scattered round the camp-fire. Even under cover of darkness, Caine and the one remaining bounty hunter would have little chance of sneaking out, grabbing the saddles and saddling up their horses without being gunned down by their attackers.

'The senator ain't gonna make it bare-back,' he growled. 'Hell, ridin' this terrain at night is dangerous 'nough, without tryin' to do it bare-back.'

'So we wait?' said Stone.

'What's the alternative?'

'We could try 'n winkle 'em out.'

'An' jest how would we do that, Jack?'

'We load both Winchesters, then I leave 'em with you an' work my way round to the far side of Three Sisters Rocks, the end opposite to where the hosses are hobbled. The distance 'tween the trees at that point an' Caine's hideaway is, I reckon, 'bout thirty yards. So, I give you a wave, an' you immediately start firin' as fast as you can. That'll keep Caine an' his pal occupied while I dash across those thirty yards an' take 'em by surprise.'

Injun Joe looked uncertainly at the Kentuckian.

'You sure you wanta do this?' he enquired. 'It's kinda risky. We could jest wait an'....'

Stone grinned. 'My patience is runnin' low, Joe. Let's git it over with here an' now,' he rasped.

The half-breed nodded. 'OK,' he said.

They quickly reloaded the two rifles and then, leaving the weapons with Injun Joe, Stone set off through the trees. He silently circled the clearing, making sure he was deep enough into the forest to remain unobserved by either Senator Caine or the bounty hunter. Then, when eventually he reached the point where the trees ran up against the bluffs, he crept forward to the forest edge and gave the half-breed a discreet wave.

Injun Joe immediately commenced firing. As he did so, Stone burst out from amongst the trees and bounded across the thirty yards or so of clearing and into the boulders. Both John Caine and Gus Brown had ducked down as low as they could get, once the bullets began flying and ricocheting off the rocks. Therefore, it was not until Stone was almost upon them that the bounty hunter spotted him. Hastily, Brown brought up his Winchester and aimed it at the Kentuckian. But he was too late. Stone's Frontier Model Colt barked. Once; twice. Both slugs struck the bounty hunter in the chest, passing through his body and sending him crashing backwards against one of the larger boulders. He dropped the rifle and slid slowly down the side of the boulder, smearing it with blood as he sank to the ground. And there he sat, his back resting against the boulder, his chest stained bright crimson, and his eyes wide open and staring, yet unseeing.

Senator John Caine glanced in horror at the bloodied corpse of the last of his hired guns and promptly discarded the Winchester he had been clutching. He leapt to his feet and stuck both hands in the air.

'I surrender!' he cried. 'Don't shoot! Don't shoot!'

Stone observed that the senator, unlike Gus Brown and the others, carried no revolver on his thigh. He wore neither gun-belt nor holster, but, then, he had not expected to have to do any shooting. He had employed the six bounty hunters to do that for him. The Kentuckian gestured towards the wide open expanse between Three Sisters Rocks and the forest.

'Git movin',' he growled.

Caine opened his mouth to protest, then seemed to think better of it. He stepped out into the clearing, closely followed by the Kentuckian. Injun Joe Brady, carrying both Winchesters, came forward from amongst the trees to join them.

'So, we meet at last, Senator,' he said.

Caine stared into the half-breed's menacing black eyes and shuddered.

'You ... you don't wanta kill me,' he quavered.

'No?' said Injun Joe.

'No! Hell, I'm a senator! You kill me an' the US Government will hunt you down for sure.'

'They've already tried an' failed.'

'This time they won't. I tell you, they'll not give up. They'll ... they'll comb Montana from one end to the other.'

Injun Joe laughed contemptuously.

'I ain't aimin' to stay in Montana. I figure, once I've done what I gotta do, I'll mosey on up into Canada, mebbe even as far as the Yukon.'

Pale and sweating, and trembling with fear, Caine tried one last, desperate plea.

'Look, I'm truly sorry for what we done. It was Jake Richards who started it. He allus was a horny ole devil. Then, after he'd tumbled yore wife, I ... I guess we all got caught up in a kinda madness an'....'

'Even although Bright Feather was big with child?'

'Yeah. It ... it was a terrible thing to do, I realize

153

that now. An' … an' I'm eager to make amends.'

'Amends?'

'That's right. I'm a rich man. You jest name a sum. Anythin' you like. Ten thousand dollars. Twenty thousand. You … you state yore price.'

Again Injun Joe laughed contemptuously.

'There is no price that I will accept for the murder of my wife.'

'But we … we didn't know she was gonna die! It was jest a li'l fun we was after. We….'

'Nine of you rape a pregnant woman, an' you call that a li'l fun?' exclaimed Stone.

'That's what it seemed at the time. Now, like I jest said, I'm truly sorry for what we done.'

Injun Joe fixed the senator with a venomous stare. His face looked as though it had been carved from granite, so harsh and implacable was his expression.

'Yo're gonna be even sorrier when I have finished with you,' he snarled.

It was at that moment that the Crow Indian, Red Knife, chose to step out from the edge of the forest.

TEN

The Crow held his Winchester with its stock hard against his shoulder. It was aimed at the group, its muzzle swinging slowly from left to right and back again.

'Red Knife, what in tarnation are you doin' here?' demanded the half-breed.

'I have come to save the senator,' replied Red Knife.

'Save this sonofabitch! But you gave me yore word as a Crow brave that you....'

'The senator is a rich man. He will pay me plenty dollars to save his life.'

'That's right, Red Knife. You got my solemn word on that,' declared Caine.

'Twenty thousand?'

'Twenty thousand is fine.'

'Yo're a greedy bastard, Red Knife!' rasped Injun Joe.

'It is not for me. It is for my people. I explained earlier that life on the reservation is ...'

But Red Knife never completed his sentence, for, while he was in full flow, Stone suddenly acted. He gave Injun Joe a shove, sending him crashing into the senator. And, as the two men fell, entangled, to the ground, so Stone likewise dropped to the floor. The Crow, taken by surprise, fired at the Kentuckian and missed. His second shot grazed Stone's left shoulder. By then, however, Stone had drawn his Frontier Model Colt and was blazing away at the Indian. Four shots thudded into Red Knife. Stone's shooting was as accurate and deadly as it was quick. All four slugs ripped into Red Knife's body within a radius of three inches, and two of them struck him in the heart.

Senator John Caine, meantime, attempted to pull a long-barrelled .30 calibre Colt revolver from the shoulder rig which was hidden beneath his jacket. The gun was only half-way out, however, when Injun Joe's fist smashed into his jaw, temporarily stunning him. The half-breed, thereupon, wrested the gun from his grasp and proceeded to pistol-whip him, breaking his nose and cracking both cheekbones. Caine cried out, and fell back, moaning and groaning.

Sitting astride the semi-conscious senator, Injun Joe looked across towards the slowly expiring Crow and then at the Kentuckian.

'Red Knife swore on his honour as a Crow brave that he would not interfere!' he exclaimed.

Stone smiled wryly.

'Wa'al, when it comes down to it, the red man ain't no different from the white man. There's some you can trust an' some you cain't,' he drawled.

'D'yuh think, if 'n' Red Knife had succeeded in savin' the senator's life, he'd have given the twenty thousand dollars to his people?' asked Injun Joe.

'I don't rightly know, but I doubt it,' replied Stone.

'Me, too.' Injun Joe shook his head sadly. He was a simple soul whose word was his bond, and he felt badly let down by the Crow.

'Wa'al, anyways, thanks for standin' by me, Jack. I can never repay the debt I owe you,' he said to the Kentuckian.

'Aw, don't mention it,' said Stone.

The two men shook hands. Then, as the Kentuckian turned and headed across the clearing towards where his horse was tethered on the forest's edge, Senator John Caine stirred and cried, 'Don't go Stone! You cain't leave me in the hands of this murderin' savage! You cain't!'

'Oh, but I can,' said Stone, and he kept on walking.

Behind him, Injun Joe rammed the barrel of the .30 calibre Colt hard into Caine's chest. Then, he pulled the knife he used for skinning purposes from his belt and, leaning forward, commenced to remove the senator's scalp.

Jack Stone trotted slowly through the forest with Caine's screams ringing in his ears. Eventually, they died away, muffled by the trees, and Stone rode on down the mountain.

Dawn was only just breaking when Injun Joe Brady rode into Great Falls on his small, coal-black racing pony. He was leading a chestnut stallion, across the back of which was strapped the badly mutilated corpse of Senator John Caine. In his left hand, the half-breed clutched a tall lance. By now there were nine human scalps attached to it. Injun Joe rode up to Mooney's Saloon and tied the chestnut to the hitching-rail. Then he turned and trotted into the centre of Main Street, where he halted and plunged the lance into the ground. Thereupon, screaming out an ancient Crow victory cry, he sped off, back in the direction he had come.

It was half an hour later when Marshal Jim Bell strolled along Main Street on his way to the law office. Consequently, he was the first person to spot the lance and the body of the senator. He was counting the scalps when the mayor, an early riser who invariably took a morning constitutional before breakfast, hustled up and joined him.

'What in tarnation's happened?' cried the mayor.

'Seems Injun Joe Brady has struck again,' replied Bell.

'What! Who ... who's the latest victim?'

'Senator John Caine.'

158

'Holy cow! How many scalps has that murderin' sonofabitch claimed now?' cried James Higgins.

'Nine, includin' the senator's', said the marshal.

They left the lance with its terrible trophies and walked over to where the mutilated remains of Senator John Caine hung across the back of the fine chestnut stallion. The mayor viewed the bloodied corpse with evident distaste. The colour left his face and he turned abruptly away.

'What 'bout them bounty hunters who rode out with Senator Caine? What's become of them?' he enquired.

'I dunno. Dead or alive, their scalps ain't here,' said Bell.

'That's kinda strange.'

'Mebbe.'

'Anyways, hadn't you best git a posse together an' ...'

'My jurisdiction begins an' ends here in Great Falls. You'll need to contact Sheriff Bob Blake over in Helena, though I doubt he'll catch Injun Joe Brady. The army, US marshals, an' God knows who else have all tried an' failed.'

'Somebody's gotta catch him. We simply cain't allow these killin's to continue.'

'Wa'al, I don't reckon they will.'

'Whaddya mean, Marshal?'

'I got a feelin' in my gut that Senator John Caine was Injun Joe's last victim.'

The marshal had made a few discreet enquiries

since his conversation with Jack Stone, and had discovered that no fewer than five of Injun Joe Brady's victims had joined Caine on his hunting party in the fall of 1897. He rather suspected the other three had also been part of that expedition. Consequently, he had come to a certain, rather unpalatable conclusion. But, as he had no definite proof, he had no intention of voicing it.

'You care to take a bet on that?' demanded the mayor.

Marshal Jim Bell smiled bleakly.

'I guess. Today's the first of June. If there ain't no more killin's by this time next year, you pay me, let's say, ten dollars. If, on the other hand, Injun Joe does murder someone 'tween now an' then, I pay you. How does that suit?'

'Yo're on,' said James Higgins.

In the event, Marshal Jim Bell was proved right. The legend of Injun Joe Brady lived on for several more years, but the killings ceased forthwith and forever. And, on 1 June 1884, the mayor of Great Falls honoured his wager and paid the marshal the ten dollars he owed him.